ROWANY DE VERE
AND A FAIR
DEGREE OF FROST

NP Novellas

ROWANY DE VERE AND A FAIR DEGREE OF FROST

Chaz Brenchley

NewCon Press
England

First published in the UK May 2025 by
NewCon Press
41 Wheatsheaf Road,
Alconbury Weston,
Cambs, PE28 4LF

NPN24 (limited edition hardback)
NPN25 (paperback)

10 9 8 7 6 5 4 3 2 1

ISBN:

978-1-914953-96-5 (hardback)
978-1-914953-97-2 (paperback)

Cover layout and design by Ian Whates
Editorial meddling and typesetting by Ian Whates

O∏E

It was the second Christmas of the year, and – as Second Christmas so often does, those years that it happens at all – it was falling deep in the chill of the long Martian winter. All across Charter territory, canals were frozen hard. Children were delighted. Snow lay heavily on the hills, more lightly across the plains: enough, but not too much. There was sledging, there were snowball fights. There would be no more school for a fortnight, and even then it might be delayed if more snow came during the Twelve Days. Meanwhile there was the promise of distant relatives making their journeys unhindered by storm or slush, bringing gifts and treats and tales of far-flung corners of the colony, cousins to play with and heroes to admire.

A frozen canal is no impediment to travel, if the

snow doesn't lie too deep. Ingenious machines built for the purpose steamed and chugged their way along that cold clear road on toothed metal wheels that bit into ice as readily as oars catch hold of water, from Elysium Field where the aetherships land to Marsport proper. Almost to Marsport, that is to say. To the city's very edge, at least, where the aldermen had decreed that all traffic should surcease for the duration. After that, passengers newly arrived from Earth – still bewildered by the voyage, many of them, still unsure how much time had passed or how they could have landed at Christmastide when they lifted from the Isle of Man at Whitsun – found themselves ushered off those curious ice-cars and packed into regular road-running charabancs to be ferried through swept city streets to their hotels, their barracks or their homes.

Excepting as always Cassini the crater-city, which is the very exemplar of exception, the major settlements of Mars have tended to grow up at junctions where one canal intersects another, the crossroads of the new world.

Not so Marsport. Marsport is the unintentional city, the earliest foundation, happening to grow where the seed fell. The first brave souls – soldiers and scientists, largely – marched off the first aethership, not honestly knowing where they'd come to or whether they'd ever see Earth again. Finding themselves canalside on a blasted plain, they marched until sundown, and then camped on the edge of the water. And there they stayed, finding no great reason to move any farther in those first days and weeks; and there Marsport grew, and there it remains in all its sordid vigour, with the canal slicing a clean edge to its growth.

Gentlemen from India – the regiments and the Service both, for once united – bade fair to call that canal the Trunk, but others considered that clumsy and frankly a little inappropriate. Mars was a fresh beginning, not an offshoot of the Raj. There is still another name in waiting; should Her Majesty ever come to visit, it will be renamed the Queen's Way, and she will be cheered from both banks for as long as she keeps to the water. Until that happy and unlikely day, it is and always will be the Grand Canal, and why not, when Marsport is so often called the Red Venice, with all her side-canals and backwaters and bridges?

Like many an edifice public or private, military or governmental or very much neither of those, the Blue Dolphin fronts onto a street – only the uncharitable curl their lip and call it an alley – and backs onto a waterway, with access from either. In this season, the intrepid leave their ice-skates by the door and come through to the lobby in borrowed slippers, shedding snow and furs and leather gauntlets as they come, calling loudly for hot buttered rum, Tommie, and a seat by the fire for God's sake or ere their fingers snap off and drop into the coals.

Strangers to the company sit farther off, more quietly.

"Mr Leonov? My name's Rowany de Vere, from the Colonial Service. I'm here to take you out."

He glanced up, visibly startled by the voice, by the name, by the long slender fingers that laid a card neatly before him.

"A girl?" he growled. "They sent a girl to me? To me…?"

"They did indeed – with all that that implies." She met his anger with an easy equanimity, taking a seat without invitation, smiling across the little table. Willing to be friends, but not actually needing to be. All she needed was his cooperation, and she knew how to win that. She hoped she did.

"I want Colpert," he said flatly.

"Yes, sir. Many people do. Nevertheless, the office sent me."

"A girl in men's clothes," he said derisively.

"A girl in winter clothes," she corrected, with the patience that years of school had taught her. "We all wear trousers, at this time of year."

He dismissed that with the contempt that it deserved, and returned to his theme: "I had his promise. I have his promise. He would come himself, he said. Colpert himself. He persuaded me, and he promised me. That is why I agreed, why I have taken the risks to come here." He couldn't keep his eyes from moving, left and right. He knew just enough to have chosen a seat in the corner, his back to the wall; not that it would do him much good, she thought, to watch his doom approaching, if it came. That's the trouble with corners: no way out.

"Mr Colpert sends his regrets," she improvised. "He's been unavoidably detained. He'll catch up with us later, if all goes well. In the meantime, I do enjoy his full confidence. He said so expressly, that I should make that clear." Was that actually her first lie, her first professional lie, told live in the field? She thought perhaps it was. Colpert was a legend on three planets, the very definition of his trade made flesh; he was popularly believed to be immortal, omniscient, untouchable. He could have had the top job, head of the table, everyone knew that; but he preferred to keep his feet on the ground and his head in the air, not to stray too close to a filing cabinet, and to have no use for the Viceroy's private number. That was understood, axiomatic. Rowany was almost sure that she had seen him, once, from the back and disappearing into a crowd. That was truly all she knew, her closest contact with the man. Her own supervisor, who had actually given her this mission, was… less ethereal. Sometimes she found it hard to imagine him doing street work at all, he was so solid and portly and seemingly welded to his desk.

This man now, her subject, her task: he might be a Colpert of a kind – he must be something special, or why would Colpert himself have taken such an interest? – but that would be on Venus or in Moscow, in St Petersburg, in the corridors of the Winter Palace. Here it would need some kind of magic to make him evanesce. What she was here for.

"You are my Uncle Vasiliy – my adoptive uncle, obviously," she said, "my father's oldest friend – and we are travelling together to New Victoria. You'll be safe there. I just have to get you that far." She surveyed him thoughtfully, and added, "You'll need to shave the beard."

"In this weather?"

"Yes please, Mr Leonov."

"That is not my name."

"No, of course not. Neither is Vasiliy Korchoi, but that's what I'm going to call you, as soon as we leave here. That's what your new papers say. You call me Rowany, which as it happens is my name. And I really am taking you home to my father. He's General Sir Charles de Vere, but you two were at school together and you still call him Infant, for all that he's older than you are. I'll explain all that later. Meantime, please, the beard?"

"This is the English madness, to go bare-faced into the winter."

"Be that as it may. I understand that you will never look English, but a little visible Englishness would help enormously. Bowing to local customs, and so forth. Military men may sport a moustache – my father does, for one; I have photographs to show you – but that's not what we have on your papers. You're not a soldier, you're an academic, specialising in the study of the Russian diaspora. Emphasis on the Martian communities, obviously. You've been here to observe the chess tournament, of course, but now you're coming home with me for a traditional English Christmas."

"I have a scar on my cheek. They know. If I remove the beard, it will only be easier to identify me."

"Mr Leonov, by the time I've finished with you, your own mother wouldn't identify you. I do know what I'm doing. Now, if you please? Go up to your room, pack anything you really want to keep, take off the beard and come down. I'll meet you at the foot of the stairs, and we'll go out the back way."

"I have my bill to pay."

"That's already attended to. Wrap a scarf around your face when you come back. You'll want it as soon as we step outside, and I'd prefer the staff here not to see you clean-shaven. You weren't to know, but this is a house of... a certain reputation. Your colleagues – your former colleagues, I should say – keep tabs on those who come here, in hopes of a blackmail opportunity. They don't find one, but persistence is a spy's first virtue; they do keep trying. And everybody loves Tommie, but that's the trouble. He's intimate with all his regulars, and as indiscreet as any bar-boy ever was. Cross his palm with half a sovereign, he'd tell anybody anything. He sees no reason not to... Tommie! There you are. I was just saying you're the best waiter in town. Bring me my usual, there's a dear, while Mr Leontov goes up to pack."

Confidence and competence: those were her watchwords, and the only way to carry this off. Even so, she was still only twenty-three, and this was her first real mission. Her first solo mission. She couldn't blame him for his visible doubts and reluctance.

She did know exactly what he saw, when he glowered at her from beneath those heavy Slavic brows. She looked younger even than she was, by the standards of Earth – or worse, of Venus. She had the native-born Martian's pale complexion and ridiculous length of limb; she must overtop him by six inches, and he would not be used to thinking of himself as a short man. She still kept her blonde hair in a schoolgirl's ponytail for preference, for convenience and speed. Her contemporaries at Oxford had laughed at her for that; her new masters encouraged her, while making sure that she knew a dozen other ways to wear it.

He still showed no signs of moving from his seat,

still less of trusting her. He lifted the card she had flourished at him, the card that still delighted her; he sniffed it, and glowered at her balefully. "This is newly printed. I can smell the ink."

"That's right, it's barely dry yet. And it's not official issue; the Colonial Office is strangely reluctant to distribute formal acknowledgements of its agents. It's only that I passed a printing press on my way here, and I had time in hand, and I couldn't resist. Have you seen the Frost Fair yet? Because you really should. I can take you that way – it is absolutely what my Uncle Vasiliy would want to see – and I don't suppose you've anything like it on Venus."

"I spent my childhood in Moscow," he said dourly. "I have seen more ice than you can possibly imagine."

"Actually, I doubt that. As a graduation present and a welcome home, my loving parents sent me on a month's expedition to the Pole" – as Martians do, she spoke as though there were only one, for the South Pole lay far outside Charter lands, and no acknowledged human foot had ever trod there, nor ever should – "in, as it happens, the very dead of last winter. Just me and a dozen squaddies, under the command of a subaltern younger than I was. It took half the journey just to train the poor boy not to blush when he spoke to me. When he had to. Public schools will do that to a lad. But anyway, I'll back one of our Martian winters against anything you have on Earth, for general ice and snow and inhospitable manners. The Frost Fair is fun, though, and the crowds will be useful, just in case we're followed."

Privately, she thought that almost certain. Her man here might be possessed of many virtues – he almost certainly possessed useful information, which was of course why her masters wanted him – but discretion was hardly one of them. The Tsar's men must have been looking for him from the moment he went missing; and he chose to come here of all places, which the Okhrana kept under surveillance anyway; and he didn't so much as think to take his beard off before he came.

Oh yes, she expected there to be a watch by now on both doors, front and back. But she did expect also to spot any tail within minutes. Her training both here and on Earth had been like a codicil to a lifelong watchfulness. This was Mars: if you didn't pay attention, you could be lost between one moment and the next. You might be eaten, you might be drowned; you might be lost more literally, in a dust-storm or anywhere out in the Dry. Here in Marsport you might be robbed or abducted or murdered, if you strayed into the wrong alley or looked at someone the wrong way. Every Martian child grew up alert, and Rowany had been given every reason to keep more alert than most. The simple possession of brothers would have been enough, even without her father's keen engagement.

One last long stare, eye to eye, and her calm patience won out – at least for now – over his resentful intransigence. He grunted sourly, got to his feet and stomped off up the stairs. She huffed a quick relief, then smiled at Tommie as he brought her drink. Campari and soda – an indulgence here, but it was a taste she'd acquired at Oxford and at least the soda water was locally made, even if the Campari had to be imported at ruinous expense. She was working on her employer's shilling here, with a generous allowance; she tossed coins onto the boy's tray, and added her customary generous tip. Keeping Tommie happy was worth the money, even when it came out of her own pocket.

She sat, and sipped, and waited. Patience held no charms, but it was absolutely part and parcel of her character, deeply inculcated. She had practised it all her life, and she could practise it now. At the same

16

time, she was practising old habits and new skills, watching the hotel lobby, testing her judgement against her knowledge against the briefing she'd received. Judgement came from a lifetime of being herself, with all that that implied; knowledge came mostly from gossiping with Tommie; the briefing had been fussy, detailed and disapproving, as was classic from the Colonial Office.

Something hush-hush had happened here at the Blue Dolphin years and years ago, before Rowany was born. Even she, with all her contacts and her connections, with all her wiles, had been unable to discover quite what that was; but the place had been known already – almost famous already, if disrepute could amount to a certain quality of fame – as a haunt of inverts. For whatever mysterious reason they'd been recruited to help, and whatever it was that they did, it was understood that they now carried immunity against the very laws that were drawn up against them. All through the Empire now it was known that homosexuals were safe on Mars, at least from prosecution. So of course they came; and sometimes it seemed to Rowany that they all came here to the Blue Dolphin. It had been one of her training exercises, to sit here and identify who was and who was not. Tommie always knew, even when the Department didn't; she had made a game of it with him, gambling pennies and favours back and forth, building trust and a sense of play between them. As her mentors had always stressed, you never knew what passing investment might pay dividends down the road.

Even today, she might have prevailed on Tommie to give her a room and privacy for an hour, to put some of her new skills to work on her client's appearance. That would have spelled a permanent change to their understanding, though; he did not currently think of her as a girl who took hotel rooms with strange gentlemen by the hour, and she hoped he never would. Besides, she preferred to get moving as soon as might be. By now she expected to be followed anyway, and taking extra time for extra measures wouldn't help with that. Even waiting while he shaved his beard might be too long a delay – but she could work better and far more quickly with a clean canvas, and she'd never shaved a man herself.

She made a mental note to pass that little moment of wisdom on to her trainers, that women in their employ should be taught to use a razor at need; it would be a handy skill, and it seemed to have escaped their attention. Like a number of other attributes handy to an agent in the field, skills not customarily the province of the fairer sex. That was really the core of the problem; the customs of the Department were the customs they had brought with them from Home, and attitudes on Mars could still confound them. Such as having female agents who expected to be treated and trained – and used – on a par with the men.

This was her first formal assignment, and – good grief, how long did it take a man to take his beard off? Patience was all very well, but the longer he kept her waiting, the harder her job would be hereafter. Did he not understand that his life was on the line here? Hers too, if it came to that, but she didn't imagine that would weigh too heavily with him. Probably not worth mentioning.

She was this close – *this* close – to marching up to his room and taking charge of his most intimate toilet, if that was what it took, when at last there was a bulky shadow on the stairs and down he came, suitcase in hand. Whatever was in that case, she'd best look through it at the earliest opportunity; frankly, she expected to be dumping it at the same time. If there weren't useful or incriminating papers in there, there was nothing that she needed or would be expected to preserve. He'd already left wife and children behind; he could leave his mementoes, his teddy bear, his underwear, whatever it was that he thought too precious to lose. His life would be prize enough, if she could manage that. She was already certain that he could not.

His jowled face was at least smooth-shaven now. That gave her something she could work with. And, as promised, he had a savage scar on the left cheek. Too crude for Heidelberg. Perhaps they should have given him a background in the military after all? Perhaps that much might even have been true.

But this was Mars, and many a civilian carried many a scar. No one would look twice, except those who were looking already. Forewarned, she would have had something in her bag to turn even their eyes away; even now, she could improvise. But not yet. The first thing was to get him moving, more urgently than he seemed to understand.

"This way, Mr Leontov. Button up your overcoat, and follow me. I don't suppose you've been out this way, have you? It's really skaters only, I'm afraid: there's no towpath on this side of the canal, the buildings open straight out onto the water. Onto the ice, I should say, at this time of year."

"Then why are we going this way? I have no skates."

"No, I didn't imagine that you would. A delegation of chess masters and their entourage, coming from Venus in a spirit of cautious reconciliation: no one would expect you to go swooping around the city the way we do in midwinter. Actually, no one would allow you to. I'm still impressed that you managed to evade our watchdogs as well as your own, to get away like this. You must tell me just how you managed it, once we're settled." That had been very much stressed at the briefing; her superiors were eager to learn what trick had so embarrassed some of their finest agents, in their highest state of alert. "I take it that you do skate, though?" Rowany went on. "After growing up with more ice than I can possibly imagine?"

"Not since I was a child," he said sourly. "There is no ice on Venus."

"No, of course. Not to worry, though; it'll come back to you soon enough. It's quite like riding a bicycle."

"I have never ridden a bicycle."

Her peal of genuine laughter surprised them both. "No bikes on Venus either? I suppose not, all things considered. Still, I didn't mean it literally. It's a skill that your body remembers all your life, I think, even if your head thinks you've forgotten how to do it. Cycling, and skating too. I expect."

Along the narrow passage, bypassing kitchen and scullery and the boot-boy's sordid lair, and here was the back-door lobby: hung with staff coats and outdoor gear, with ice skates jumbled promiscuously beneath the benches on either side, and more tied neatly into pairs and hung by their laces from pegs in the wall.

Rowany retrieved her own skates from one of those pegs, then surveyed the others thoughtfully between glances at her client's feet.

"Try these on for size," she said briskly, hooking down a pair with well-greased leathers and apparently sharp blades.

"Whose are these?"

Of course he was going to be difficult, in this as in everything. She suppressed a sigh, and continued her policy of honesty-when-possible. "I haven't the faintest idea. Some gentleman who takes care of his skates, and will be upset to find them gone, I imagine. I'll make that right another day, as best I can. Right now we really need to hurry, please."

Russians, she was learning, do not respond as readily as Englishmen to nursery briskness with its hint of scolding. Nevertheless, he sat on a bench and began to unlace his boots. She did the same – briskly,

22

yes, her fingers both more nimble and more accustomed to the work. He had at least brought the right clothes for the season, and his own boots were good enough to carry with them; but heavy leather boots couldn't possibly be Venus wear, to judge by all she'd heard of that steaming acrid hell. These shone with polish, and the stitches stood out boldly against the unscuffed hide; they looked barely worn at all. In addition to rediscovering childhood ways with laces, he must surely also be rediscovering the childhood pain of blisters and feet rubbed raw.

The stranger's skates might even be more comfortable, once he'd found his balance and remembered how to glide. They did seem to fit well enough, at least. She took swift possession of his discarded boots, knotted the laces together and looped them amiably about his neck; then she did the same with her own; and then she extended a friendly hand.

"Up you come, Uncle Vasiliy. Lean on me as much as you need to, until you find your feet out there. Don't worry, I'm very springy; I won't let you fall. By the way, I suspect I used to call you 'Uncle Silly' when I was littler, when you used to come and visit my parents just so you could play with me. Don't be surprised if I fall back into childish ways and let that slip out a time or two…"

Out on the ice, and true to her guess, he needed her elbow for a while but not too long. Even once he'd got into his stride, though, he still needed her to carry his suitcase. That would be ammunition for her, when it came to the argument about leaving it behind somewhere unobtrusive. Or possibly somewhere thoroughly obtrusive, to lay a false scent. She was a skilled hare-and-hounds runner; she knew many ways to deceive a chase.

This wasn't a game, of course – and yet, and yet. The same principles surely applied, whatever the stakes. She did still need to check what was in the case, but already she was thinking of it more as scent than burden.

Right now they were being followed, too close for any misleading scent to send the pursuit off-track. One man ahead and one behind, and she thanked her lucky stars for recent and explicit training; she'd never have spotted the front-tail else, would never have thought to look for it.

Very well: they were spotted, known and hemmed in, fore and aft. Nevertheless. She didn't think he knew that, her Uncle Vasiliy pro tem – which was all to the good, in all honesty. She could handle him better if he wasn't half panicked, always staring over his shoulder or trying to second-guess the path ahead.

Not that she had the first idea of the path ahead, just now. She recalled her mentor, in her first week of lectures, when it still felt a lot like school and university: *When in doubt, trust your instincts. Don't try to force matters along, don't try to out-think the situation. Follow your natural path, and trust that an opportunity will find you.*

Very well, then. She was out on the ice with her beloved Uncle Silly; of course she'd want to show him the Frost Fair. Or show him herself, rather, being an adult at the Frost Fair. He must have seen her here as a child, often and often: hurling balls and sliding pucks, greedy for prizes; guzzling fairy floss and humbugs, greedy for treats. Shouting and falling – less often as time went by, and when did she last fall on ice, whether she had skates or not? – and laughing, always laughing, hurrying, dragging him ahead. Always greedy for fun.

Very well, then. Of course she'd want him to see her as a grown-up now, sophisticated in her pleasures – but of course part of being a grown-up was letting your early child self shine through, revisiting the simpler games and treats of yesteryear. She wasn't quite sure what the Russian was for 'yesteryear', and hoped she wouldn't have to explain.

Gliding along at the best pace he could manage – she could have skated circles around him as they went, and almost wanted to do it, but she really wasn't twelve any longer and he might not understand – they followed this shadowed narrow side-channel down to the Pool, where empty wharfs and jetties spoke of absent shipping, all far to the south now in search of open water and safe docking. Marsport was still busy, still the grubby avaricious heart of provincial life – but not here, not until the thaw.

Up another, broader way, and here were more people sliding in from one side and the other till they were almost a crowd, almost united in their shared purpose. Here was the final water-gate, frozen open; and here at last they debouched onto the Grand Canal itself: wider than any river back on Earth, too wide for any bridge, so wide that the settlement on the far bank was another town entirely, no part of Marsport proper.

Now there were so many people pressed so close she was at risk of losing track of their watchers ahead and behind; she could almost hope already that they might lose track of her and her charge. Almost.

Keeping close to the bank was instinctive, a native Martian habit. Even the great blazing bonfire on the ice that marked this end of the Frost Fair mile was practically under the shadow of the houses looming above. Daredevil children might skate all the way across, yes, and daredevil grown-ups too, for certainly the ice was safe enough; it was hard work, though – Rowany's legs still ached from yesterday's effort – with small reward waiting on the other side. Marsporters were rarely welcome in Farhome Township, and there was really little to do but turn around and skate home again, over ice still thick with snow. More than that, though, no Martian could ever feel quite comfortable too far from solid ground. Their beloved Red Planet offered many ways to die before your time, and many of those lurked in canals. The ice might be yards thick beneath her feet, the merlins might be drowsing deeply beneath the ice; it didn't matter. She might never willingly confess it to anyone except her trainers, with whom absolute openness and honesty was de rigueur, but Rowany had not enjoyed that long solitary skate one bit more than the sheer physical accomplishment of it had allowed. She knew now that she could do it, which had been half the point; she would do it again if she must; she would not do it again for any lesser compulsion.

A spirited game of ice hockey was going on beyond the fire, and she could make out solitary skaters and courting couples even beyond that, far out in the gloaming. Nevertheless, so long as she was in charge – which she absolutely was, despite his grumbles, so long as she could keep up the initiative and the tempo, *keep him moving, don't give him time to think* – they'd keep with the crowds and the lights, close in to the bank. There was no safety out there; darkness and isolation were seductive, which meant dishonest. Untrustworthy. That was inherent. These shadows fore and aft might be more than mere watchers, might be assassins primed and lethal. That was almost the hardest lesson to absorb, for one who knew never to trust Mars, but who had always trusted Martians.

She was trusting Martians now: trusting them to pack in close on every hand, trusting them to be their traditionally awkward, balky selves. She knew how to filter through a crowd of them, using her height and her sex shamelessly, her elbows, even her skates if necessary. She could tow her client through in her shadow. If their pursuers were Russian, though, as she devoutly hoped, they were likely to find themselves left behind, and they ought to be grateful for that, though they wouldn't know it. The alternative didn't bear thinking about, even if it would be a gift to her and her charge. Martians *en fête* were only ever one injudicious shove away from a riot. They'd take it from a girl, so long as she was careful about it, perhaps a little flirty, and clearly one of their own. From a man and an evident stranger, new to Mars and Martian manners, they absolutely would not.

Half of them might live in cities now, it might be as much as half, but they were still a pioneer people at heart, her people: stone-certain, iron-hard with themselves and each other, carefully courteous day-to-day because your neighbours might be all that was keeping you alive tomorrow but still boisterous now and then, when they thought they could afford to be, when nothing worse than a bad head and an empty purse come morning seemed to threaten them.

Boisterous now, then. City and country cheek by jowl, here for the Frost Fair or the holidays or entirely at home; old folk and whippersnappers, ladies and lumberjacks, pickpockets and professors and the colonial police. Ice is, as they say, the great leveller: it brings everybody down. And fairy floss brings them all to the fair.

Rowany didn't actually care that much for spun sugar any more, somewhat to her own surprise. She was all too aware that childhood delights were a fading pleasure, but did they honestly have to fade so quickly?

No matter: this was not the time to be pining over her lost innocence. Not that she'd ever been exactly innocent, thinking back. Lost mischief would be more apposite: as far as she remembered, her early years had been entirely a tale of wickedness, fuelled by humbugs and fudge. But let the dead past bury its dead; her task now was to keep her present company alive.

Oh, and herself, that too.

Crowds thinned just a little once they were past the bottleneck of the bonfire, once the actual stalls opened up on either side, drawing attention and custom away from the central thoroughfare.

Here indeed there was room enough for a man to stand and let the stream of traffic divide about him, while he held out half a dozen sticks of spun sugar in clouds of pink and white: "Fairy floss, ladies! Buy it for your kids, buy it for yourselves! Fairy floss! Penny a stick! You'll take one, won't you, miss?"

That last was aimed directly at Rowany, the price of bright and visible interest. In fact she'd only been smiling from nostalgia, and the private pleasure of a prophecy come true. Of course the first fairground attraction they encountered had to be a fairy-floss seller. She had pictured him in her head and here he was, with his gaudy clothes and his lopsided grin and yes, absolutely his attraction, although there was something in his dark eyes that she really didn't want to probe. Fairy floss came from fairy folk, so far as child-Rowany was concerned; that was enough.

She shook her head regretfully – genuinely regretful – and took advantage of the moment and the space ahead to spin on her heel and skate backwards for a yard or two. She might have been checking on her uncle, to be sure he was keeping up; she might have been showing off, for the man who was keeping up but only laboriously so; in fact she was looking past him, looking for their pursuit. And seeing no sign of the face that had followed them since the Blue Dolphin but certainly something of a kerfuffle some distance back, where an impatient man might indeed have tried to barge his way through the crowd and found himself abruptly flat on his back, with menacingly sharp blades all about him and menacing voices overhead.

Ah, her people: always willing to rise to an occasion. And she needn't even feel guilty, for she'd done nothing to provoke the incident; it was entirely down to him.

That still left the front tail, who was exploiting the crowd more cleverly, using it to slow himself down, to keep him handily and credibly in touch with those he watched. Very well: she could afford to do the same, perhaps, for a little while. Certainly there were excuses all around them.

"Uncle Vasiliy! You wouldn't want fairy floss, I think – but shall we get some chestnuts? Look, there's a brazier over there, and they're so good hot from the fire." Hot enough that you had to toss them hand to hand, you couldn't hold them for long enough to peel, never mind bite. And when you could, when you did bite, the burn of it brought tears to your eyes but still, it had that irresistible savoury sweetness, sharpened with salt crystals that tried to bite you back; and she knew all the stories about the terrible lives of the salt miners and their kin, and she was duly shocked and oh so duly grateful...

That, now: that was a proper Russian scowl, black and foreboding. "This is not the time," he growled crushingly. "How can you be so foolish?" And he glanced back over his shoulder, with enough tight-lipped anxiety that she wondered if he had spotted the tail after all.

Happily, Rowany remained uncrushed. "Don't be silly, Uncle Silly. This is exactly the time." She seized his arm and steered him expertly through the streams of passers-by, this way and that. Years of experience came back to her, helping girls new to school, new to ice, sometimes new to Mars entirely. "Who comes to the fair and doesn't stop for chestnuts, or for hoop-la, or for a ride on the merry-go-round? If anyone's looking for you here," still hedging her bets against his hoped-for lack of awareness, "the quickest way to draw their eye would be to bully our way through all unheeding of what's around us. Don't worry, I will see you safe – but it would help if I could see you smile first. We're supposed to be having fun out here."

She allowed him to pay for the chestnuts, with pennies counted carefully one by one into the seller's hand; but she insisted on carrying the bag herself. That had always been a significant part of the treat, warmth stealing through paper and gloves into her fingers, hotter and hotter, becoming almost too hot to hold, almost. Only then of course you had to pass them on, because you needed both hands free if you actually wanted to eat one. That was what brothers were for, and their best use in her estimation: big and loud and occasionally convenient, occasionally justifying their interminable presence in her otherwise satisfactory family life.

Her charge now was big and – she was sure – could be loud when he chose. She wasn't yet sure of his convenience, occasional or otherwise. She decided to keep the chestnuts in one hand, him in the other, until they found a place where she could put both down and depend on them to stay there.

Too wise to rack her brains for fear of out-thinking herself, she left the discovery of that place to happenstance, coasting along from one stall to the next, until –

Here it was, that place of happenstance: place of a happy meeting, only hours since. Here was the press itself, a great and deliberate weight of cast iron, swung down by crane surely and set casually on the ice as though on rock, as though it could have had no thought of plunging through. Here were vertical cases of oak, as tall as she was, their every compartment stacked with characters of lead, which was surely over-egging the pudding. And that wasn't even to mention the counter, oak again, all its drawers full of paper, nor the canisters of ink. It was like a physical manifestation of her own determined motto, *confidence and competence*, oh yes.

No sign of the printer himself, nor of his beguiling ink-smeared apprentice Billy, who had actually set the type for her calling card and printed off two dozen copies, with her watching every stage over his shoulder. They'd had a Printing Club in her last year at school, but she'd been too busy to join; she could regret that now, her mind jangling with ways to use ink-and-paper technologies in her new profession. She might write to her mentors, perhaps, to suggest a new training course. These were skills that would surely come in handy, if she had them at her fingers' ends.

For the moment, she must remain dependent on other people's skills. In their absence, she abused their presumptive hospitality by setting her bag of chestnuts down on their counter, before it could scorch her entirely. She blew on her gloved fingers, more for the show of it than any relief it offered, and unscrewed the twist of paper that bound the bag shut.

"Chestnut, Uncle Silly?" And then, in an undertone, because he still looked mutinous, "Just lean on the counter, look nonchalant, and eat a few chestnuts. Please. You'll probably need to take your gloves off to handle the shells, unless you can do this." She popped one steaming nut into her mouth whole, unpeeled, a party trick she'd learned – of course! – from her occasionally useful brothers. Feeling momentarily regretful, as she always did, that her science lessons at school had never taught her how something still too hot to handle could be managed perfectly easily in the mouth, which by rights ought to be more sensitive, she worked the shell off with her teeth – Peter could do it in one piece, but Peter was an infuriating mortal even when he wasn't exuding a fatal glamour in his Double Reds lieutenant's uniform – and spat the fragments elegantly out onto the ice. One quick chew and a hard swallow, and, "You stay here, I won't be a moment."

"Wait, you are leaving...?"

"Only briefly. Don't worry, I'm only going in there," with a nod of her head to the curtained booth that lurked suspiciously behind this open-air printing shop. It had an iron chimney-pipe that was cheerfully puffing smoke out into the evening, and she was tolerably sure what she'd find inside: one printer's devil neglecting his duties, staying comfortably warm in his master's absence.

She slid around the counter and coasted quietly up to the booth, twitched the curtain aside and went boldly in, talking already, she was that confident: "Billy, I've brought you some chestnuts, just to say thank you for such a marvellous – oh. Oh, lor'. I'm most terribly sorry…"

Of course she was absolutely right, and of course she was terribly, terribly wrong. Understanding boys as she did, with all those brothers always in her hair, a lifetime of observations, she had been certain to the core of her being that Billy would be in that cosy little cave, and his employer would not. But why, oh, why had she not paused to consider that he might not be alone?

She wasn't quite sure which of the three of them was blushing most, herself looming over them or Billy on his stool or the girl on her knees before him, dabbing at his ink-stained cheek with a handkerchief.

Even through all their mutual embarrassment and confusion, Rowany's training held good. *She's no older than Billy. Cheaply but nicely dressed, everything clean, made up better than I could do it myself: she's a shop girl, but in a classier shop than she could ever afford. Or I, for that matter.*

They probably call it an establishment. Or else a boutique. And I'd guess she has younger brothers, but there isn't anything sisterly about her feelings for Billy…

The girl was scrambling to her feet now, finding her balance, finding her skates much easier to manage than her words. "I – I'm sorry, miss, but he always gets so smeary with the ink, and I know how to get it off, so…"

She was packing the handkerchief away as she spoke – or no, it wasn't quite a handkerchief, it was a square of soft fabric that had its own compartment in the very professional-looking make-up case that she was possessed of, that was interesting Rowany strangely.

"So of course you come and do that for him, when your workday is over."

"Well – yes, miss. My work's at the House of Worthing, I demonstrate the whole line of their cosmetics, and Miss Evelyn never minds if I take the samples home to practice with. My mum swears she's never looked so pretty," added with a little giggle, and a glance aside at the mute, appalled Billy.

Nobly resisting the urge to reach out and ruffle his hair, Rowany said, "Well, if you have a magic formula to take off printer's ink without an intolerable deal of scrubbing, you're worth your weight in gold hereabouts, eh, Billy-boy?"

He glowered at her, sensing himself teased, but still grunted, "Yes, miss."

"Oh, please, miss, you won't tell Mr Morris, will you? Only he might not like it, me coming here and taking Billy from his work…"

I'm sure he wouldn't – just as I'm sure you only come when you're sure he won't be here. And of course Billy never confesses. And now I have power here, though no authority; and of course I'm going to use it.

"Trust me," she said, giving away all her advantage in a moment, "I won't say a word. But tell me – oh, I'm sorry, what is your name? I'm Rowany."

"Mary, miss."

"This is Polly, miss."

They both spoke at once, she being formal and he introducing his best girl by her pet name, the one he always used, and they were endearingly confused again while she was clearer by the minute.

"Well, I'll call you Polly too, if I may, if that's what you like – and please, Polly, would you let me use your rather splendid cosmetics box there, to help me do something a little strange but very necessary?"

"Well – yes, miss, of course, but I do need to take it back in the morning, and Miss Evelyn might be a bit queer if there's too much missing…"

"Oh, don't worry. I only need to use a little of this and that. It's been our secret until now," since all of a couple of hours ago, "but Billy can tell you that I work for Authority. My work is – well, terribly hush-hush, so I'm swearing you both to secrecy right now. Suffice to say, I have to make a man look very different from the way he does now, and I need to do it quickly and quietly, and your box there will help me enormously. If you want to watch, just stand over in the corner there, the pair of you, and keep quiet."

That said, with a firmness of tone that struck awe into their wide eyes, she went outside and beckoned to her charge. "In here, please, Uncle Vasiliy."

Rather to her own surprise, and possibly to his, he came without argument. His expression was still sour and unwilling, but at least he came. She said, "Good. Sit down on the stool, where I can see you in the light. Billy, I'm sorry to cast you forth, but shouldn't you be out there manning the shop anyway?"

"Mr Morris has gone home for his supper," the boy objected, "he won't be back for another hour yet."

"All the more reason," she said, gently propelling him out, "why you should be manning the shop. You can keep yourself warm with the chestnuts on the counter there, until I call you back. No, Polly, don't you go with him. I need your expertise."

Actually she wasn't sure that she did, but she hoped that the Russian might be more amenable, or at least less resistant, with two young women attendant on him. And no male audience.

"What do you want me to do, miss?" Polly was utterly at sea, but none the less gratified. "I've never made up a man before."

"I don't suppose you have. It's much the same" – Rowany had practised often enough, during her training and since then at the Blue Dolphin, on Tommie and his clientèle – "except that he won't be used to it either. But we're not trying to disguise blemishes today, rather the opposite. I want to make that scar look like a fresh wound, raw and sore. The bigger and more obvious the better. I want him to look so horrible that people will take one glance and look away, and remember nothing about his face except the terrible accident that has left him so cruelly marked. The people trying to follow us won't be describing him like that, so it's a better disguise than anything, do you see?"

"Coo." Polly's gaze was suddenly more attentive and more professional, fixed on the Russian's face rather than her sweetheart's absence. There was more thrill than anxiety in her voice as she said, "Are there really people following you, miss?"

"There really are." Apparently it was hopeless, trying to persuade the girl to call Rowany by her name. No matter. This wasn't the first time she'd been mistaken for a grown-up; she knew how to carry it off with aplomb. "With your help and Billy's, I believe we can give them the slip. Now, what do you have there in your box of tricks...?"

Two

It took time, but there wasn't any hurry; the longer the watchers outside had to linger, the harder it would be for them to keep up any kind of cover. Marsport Police would be out there mingling with the crowd, in uniform and otherwise, keeping a weather-eye open for pickpockets and drunkards, any unwelcome behaviour. A typical night of Frost Fair should supply plenty to hold their interest, but nevertheless: she was in hopes that overt or covert interest from Authority might be enough to drive pursuit away, at least for a little while, perhaps for long enough. If not, well. Another fish would be along in a minute. That was a phrase – and an attitude – learned from her ridiculous brothers. One or another of them would occasionally condescend to take her out for a day's fishing. She didn't remember any actual fish ever being actually caught, but much of their pith and wisdom seemed to be drawn from another universe, in which trout and salmon sprang eagerly onto their virgin hooks.

It took time, much consultation, a little trial-and-error, wiping off and starting again – and a great deal of mollifying an impatient subject – but eventually Rowany could draw back the curtain and call out, "Billy, are you busy? No? Well, come in here for a minute."

Billy duly came; and stood in the doorway staring, horrified, stammering, "What – what happened? Mr Morris'll slay me, if he was hurt in here…"

Polly shrilled with delight, clapping her hands at her own cleverness. "It's just cosmetics, silly. *Maquillage*, Miss Evelyn likes to call it. Makeup to the likes of you, Billy Carnie. But you know that, we told you. It does look awful, though, don't it?"

"It looks real, is what it looks like. You're awful clever, Pol."

"Oh, Miss did it all really, I only helped a bit." Nevertheless, she bloomed under his praise. Rowany rather wanted to wrap the pair of them in cotton wool and keep them for ever, as an heirloom of sweet young love. Which only made it harder, what she had to ask of them next.

"May we go now?" The Russian's voice was as harsh as his face was now repulsive, with a living wound running from his eye to the corner of his mouth, barely scabbed over, vivid and impossible to look at, impossible not to see.

"No-o, not yet. Not quite yet. We have to assume that we were seen, coming in here. Which means there'll be a watch out there, waiting for us to come out."

"Then what was the point of all this? If they see me come out, they know who I am, without all this nonsense."

"That's why we need a diversion. Something that will clear the ice out there, in such a way that watchers would need to leave too. There's only one way I can think of to do that. Billy, for half a crown, would you be willing to go out there and call cracking? They'd believe it here, coming from you, with that great weight of the press and everything behind you."

"No, miss." It was the girl who denied her, instantly, determinedly. "Mr Morris would beat him if he did that."

Billy shrugged, as though one more beating really didn't signify in the greater scheme of things. Likely it didn't; he looked to be a lad who'd take such things in his stride. But even so, he didn't want to do it. "T'ain't the beating," he said stoutly, "but I'd lose my place, and what would my mum do then, with me back on her hands and known for a troublemaker?"

"Fair enough. I don't want to cost you trouble. Or your mum. It was just an idea. Maybe we can think of a better one."

For a moment they gazed at each other, Rowany only hoping that she didn't look as gormless as the two youngsters – but then Billy chuckled, then he grinned and snapped his fingers and said, "Hey, Pol. Remember when you were round the shop that time and I took my spanner to that rusty nut to make that noise...?"

"Yes, I do. You scared me." She made a fist and thumped him on the arm, as hard as she could manage. "I thought there was something down in the cellar, and it was coming up to eat us."

"That's right. Sounded right awful, didn't it?" Then, to the baffled Rowany, "I dunno what cracking really sounds like, miss, I've never heard it – but neither have most of them out there. And I dunno what it'll sound like out here, on ice, with water underneath. But I do know that it's a bloody – ow!" as Polly thumped him again.

"You mind your tongue with a lady, Billy Carnie. I'm very sorry, miss, he don't know no manners."

"Don't mind me," Rowany said faintly, as Billy rubbed his offended member and glowered adoringly at his girl, while he drew breath to continue his narrative.

"No, but it's a, a horrible sound, miss, and it sounds just like it's coming up through the floorboards; and that nut's still just as rusty, because Mr Morris never troubles himself to check down there. And I've got my spanner right here" – he flourished it, presumably for fear that a lady such as Rowany might not recognise the article – "and if Polly was outside in the crowd and made a fuss, then we wouldn't need to do nothing else. You don't even have to cry cracking," he went on directly to his inamorata, "just let out a scream like you did that night. Some smart-arse – I mean, some person's gonna think they know what it means, and call crack for you. Then Bob's your daisy."

"I think I could do that, miss."

"'Course you could. And then I'll just come running out and find you, and get you to the bank quick as quick, just like there really was a crack, and we'll clear the ice before you know it, miss, and no blame because it wasn't us that called it."

"Well, if you're sure you won't get in trouble…"

"I'll wait till everyone's panicking, miss – maybe I'll help them along with another squeal or two – and then Mr Morris can't put nothing on me. Maybe a bruise or two for quitting the shop, but that ain't nothing. I gets worse from Polly, any day." He grinned at her, as she shaped to thump him again.

One by one, the youngsters slipped away through the curtain. Nerves made Polly quiet, Billy jittery; Rowany hoped that they could both hold themselves together long enough to play their parts. Hope was all she had to do: hope and wait, in this claustrophobic space with the sullen silent Russian.

She warmed her hands at the redcoal stove, and waited with no hope at all for his next eruption.

"Now you are trusting my safety to children playing games!"

Yes, there it was. She sighed aloud, and didn't try to swallow it. "That's right, Uncle Vasiliy. Yours and mine too. And we may have to trust ourselves to other guardians before we're home, even less likely ones. Let's hope not, shall we? If this works, perhaps we can skate away free and clear. Hush now, I want to hear what happens…"

She didn't really need to shush him. When it came, the noise was insidious, felt as much as heard, unmissable and impossible to ignore. It set her teeth on edge, and worse: she was sure, entirely sure to the core of her Martian soul, that it came from deep within the ice beneath her. That she knew better mattered apparently not a whit. She was on her feet regardless, her breathing short and fast, ready to fling the curtain back and hurtle to safe ground.

Her companion lacked that reflex, or had lost it. The deep sepulchral groaning came again, and even now he sat stolidly on his stool, unaffected, seemingly oblivious.

He was surely alone in that. Beyond the walls of the booth she could hear screams and rush, the sounds of bodies falling or knocked down, emergency whistles and a dozen separate voices crying "Crack! It's cracking! All ashore!" and *"Sauve qui peut!"* because that was the first rule of survival on Mars, that you saved yourself first and looked to help others later. These days it might be a rule more honoured in the breach than the observance, but it was still a part of every child's training: get yourself safe, don't be a problem for someone else to solve.

'Women and children first' was an Earthbound protocol long left behind, that made no sense out here.

One last eldritch moan, and despite the rumpus out there she heard the clatter of Billy's spanner as he dropped it, as he presumably leaped out from behind the counter and ran to rescue his beloved, who presumably as a good Martian girl would already be rescuing herself quite efficiently, thank you. She wished the two of them silently well, realised that she'd forgotten to give Billy his promised half-crown and decided that was probably just as well, as he'd only have been offended by the suggestion that he was adventuring for cash. Not that he'd have refused it, but she rather liked herself for nurturing the amateur in him, encouraging him to do something for the fun of it first, and then because others were depending on him. Needing his help to get themselves safe.

"Ready, Uncle?"

"Stop calling me that, I am not your –"

But she had already twitched the curtain aside and reached back an arm; he was finally as curious as she, and he needed her arm to get safely up onto his skates again, and so he came readily enough, without even reaching the end of his complaint.

If he saw what she saw, it was a line of receding chaos, a surging retreat, the whole Earth vs Mars experience defined in a single moment. She loved her people and she loved her planet, but she and they had always known who would win in the end. Humanity had not conquered here; they had been invited, and they were here on sufferance, for so long as they were convenient and no hope of holding on longer.

On a smaller scale, though, whatever Russian observers were out there had been swept up in the crowd, either equally believing or else unwilling to expose themselves by staying out on supposedly fractured ice. Now was her time: she tugged on her charge's arm and led him out, turned their backs to the bank and started skating into the encompassing dark beyond the lamplight of the fair.

"Where are we going? There is nothing out here."

Nothing but a mile of open ice, no, and then the opposite bank, the unwelcoming community that lived there. He likely wouldn't feel the same frisson that she had, not understanding all that that open mile implied. Nevertheless, she wasn't sure that he could skate that far, and she didn't mean to find out.

"Nothing but darkness, no. Just now, darkness is our friend. If they're watching from the bank, if they can see us at all, they'll only see us disappear. They couldn't possibly follow; no one's going to be allowed back onto the ice now until it's been checked. Probably not till tomorrow, after another night of freezing. All we need to do is keep out of the light until we're well away from here. Then I'll take you by the back ways to the railway station, and we'll still be in time for the last train to New Victoria. That's a sleeper, so you can get your head down for the night. I'll send a telegram ahead, and with any luck we'll meet my father for breakfast in the Cadena."

As a plan it was light on details and dependent on matters outwith her control, but it seemed to placate her putative uncle. At least, he let his grumbling go and concentrated merely on skating. He was finding it more and more of an effort; she did her best to help him unobtrusively, linking her arm with his "because we need to stay together, and we could lose each other entirely in this darkness," gifting him something of her balance and something of her springy energy.

In honesty, there was no chance of their losing each other. All the lights and smokes and noise of the vulgar city lay away to their right in a vivid, raucous skyline. This far out it cast no more shadows at their feet than did the fugitive moons, but it gave their night-adjusted eyes enough to see everything around them. Sharp starlight alone might have done that, but Rowany was glad to have the city's smudgy silhouette as a guide and a reassurance. She had skated in the dark like this before, often and often, out for a lark with friends or family, even with her never-to-be-sufficiently-abominated brothers.

Across the abandoned hockey pitch, a wide circle around the still-blazing bonfire, not to betray themselves in its broad fall of light. Then the shadows closed in properly, and Rowany felt bolder, letting her feet bring them in towards the high bank. Still at an angle, to be still farther away from any presumptive watchers before she chanced even the narrowest and least populated side channels.

Marsport had never been home, but she had visited often, staying with school or family friends for holidays, more recently passing through on her way to Earth and back to home again, Oxford years and training. She knew – mostly from her schoolgirl friends, and their own disreputable brothers – all the hidden ways to get around, on foot or bikes or skates as children do: the bridges and the weirs, the alleys and the backwaters, the labyrinthine paths that any unplanned city generates and Marsport more than most.

Now she brought all that cryptic knowledge into play, ducking this way and that, keeping away from lighted buildings and public thoroughfares, lingering in the shadows of warehouses while mobs of merrymakers passed by, once squeezing herself and her companion breathlessly behind a frozen lock gate when she saw a lamp approaching. When the light went by without pausing, she could make out two policemen, skating swiftly: a regular patrol or a sudden errand, she couldn't tell. She might have called after them, she might have asked for help; that calling card seemed suddenly less foolish, potentially actually of use. It might at least buy her an escort to the station and then a minute of time with their superiors, long enough to make a phone call that would carry its own conviction.

Pride held her tongue, though, unless it was distrust. Men might don police uniform who were not themselves policemen. Searchers, say, scanning the back ways for two eagerly sought fugitives. Better to be cautious, then, or prideful. Better at any rate to rely on her own skills, her own knowledge, her areas of certainty. No man's survival should be predicated on her areas of doubt. No man's, and certainly not her own.

Very well, then. She held her charge back against the slick ice-covered stone of the lock wall, with the great wooden gate just inches from their noses – just as cold, just as hard as the wall – and watched the seeming policemen vanish with only a passing regret. She was still in charge of the situation, still on top. They had lost their watchers, they were nearly at the railway station and only a safe night's travel from her mission's end…

Out now from the shadow of the gate, and on: and here was a narrow flight of steps on their right, between two flanking sides of brick that rose up and up into windowless walls. Those were engine-houses, and just ahead were the train-docks where cargoes were transferred between rail and canal. Here was where they left the ice, because these steps would lead them through to the passenger concourse by ways not dedicated to the public, meant for railway workers only and used – of course! – by bold children and occasionally the adults they grew into.

Rowany supposed that the fun of going where she really wasn't supposed to would ebb eventually –

but not yet, apparently. Maturity would be as unwelcome now as chastity to Saint Augustine. Besides, she had wholly legitimate reasons for taking this path today, and was delighted to have it in her private gazetteer of the city. The nostalgic thrill of trespass was no more than icing on the cake.

"Sit down on the steps here, Uncle Vasiliy, and we'll take our skates off. Shanks' pony for us now."

"Shanks? Pony? Who is Shanks?" He looked up as though expecting to see a ride waiting at the top of the stairs.

"Oh – sorry, no. It's an expression. It means we walk now. Not for very far, though. Just through to the platforms and onto the train. Loop your skates' laces over the hand-rail here; there's no point carrying them any farther, when we won't be needing them again. New Victoria is not a water city like Marsport." Nor did New Victoria have urchins lurking at every corner, watching every passer-by, ever ready to snatch whatever offered. Anything abandoned here would find its way swiftly to a new owner. There was a kind of commons of the canal, a whole other layer of society living beside or below the upper echelon, parasitic upon it – or no, symbiotic rather, making its own contributions to the good of the whole. They also serve who only take and share, and Marsport would not be the same without its underclass of thieves and rogues and vagabonds. And spies.

The Russian took his time pushing feet into boots and lacing them up again, but at last he was ready.

"Up we go, then. Hold fast to the rail, these steps are thick with ice. When we reach the top, stay close. There are trains coming and going all the time, and we have to cross a lot of tracks."

"I have eyes in my head," he growled. She wondered if he was always so gruff and ill-tempered, or if sustained fear and uncertainty had put him out of sorts.

"That's good," she said mildly. "Make sure to use them, then. We can watch out for each other."

Hearing something behind, below – a whistle soft as a whisper, the scrape of steel on ice, perhaps a murmur – she paused at the head of the steps, and looked back.

Sure enough: two shadowy figures were there already, claiming their skates. Rowany felt a brief pang for the loss of her own, which had been hers since school, well loved and well treated, moulded by long use exactly to the shape of her feet. They'd only be in the way, though, in these next hours, and skates could be replaced. Perhaps she'd treat herself to a handmade pair, as a reward for mission accomplished.

Besides, those kids down there looked hungry. If they weren't so bundled up in accumulated coats against the weather, they'd be even leaner than they seemed. One glanced up, raising a hand in thanks. Rowany waved back, then took the Russian's elbow and steered him the way that he should go.

There came another whistle rising from the ice below, much more definite, distinct, a phrasing that she knew: *these are friends*, it said, *let them pass*. Winter was hard on alley children, with slimmer pickings to be begged even from the generous and fewer potential victims among the unwary, pockets much more difficult to pick beneath layers of fur and leather. Open gifts won easy friendships. Rowany was under no illusions as to that friendship's durability, but if it lasted the next half-hour she'd take it gladly. Two adults together should stand in no danger here – but desperation can drive even children into folly, and a savage Martian winter can drive any creature desperate. When sandcats prowl city streets in search of strays, a stray urchin with a belly full of empty may well carry a hoarded knife out hunting, aye, and use it too.

Confidence and competence. Very well. She would be

confident that she had bought their favour, at least for this little time; she would be competent in her guidance through the maze ahead and her delivery of her subject first to the right platform for their train, and then safe home tomorrow.

Yes.

"This way, Uncle V. There really isn't a path, but I know every twist and every turn from here, I used to come here when I was a wicked schoolgirl let loose in the big city, with playmates my parents would certainly have disapproved of if they'd only known. Sometimes with my brothers too, but that's another story." She only mentioned this because it was somehow easier to keep him moving if she kept her tongue moving at the same time, an almost meaningless narrative that oiled the way against his obstinate resistance, his apparent determination to stop at every corner, to gaze about him and want to go that way and not this, or to ask another crushing question that challenged her competence, or…

A devil-bug droned by her ear; a brick cracked in the bitter cold.

Wait.

A devil-bug in the deep winter, in the heart of the city? Devil-bugs don't outlive the first frost, and don't leave the desert anyway.

Bricks don't crack like that, one brick abruptly in the middle of a wall.

Wait…

THREE

She was too slow. Even as she gaped at the wall, at the broken brick, at the star-shatter pattern of it, the Russian hit her hard and low, bringing her crashing down onto elbows and knees.

It should have been me. She knew it, acknowledged it, even as she fell. It should have been her bringing him down, doing her job; it should have been her – *confident and competent, yes* – and not him saying, fairly calmly, "That was a bullet. They have found us."

She was briefly impressed with how swift he'd been to know it, and to react. At the same time she was resentful, because the speed of his response only underscored the slowness of her own. She could perhaps reassure herself with the thought that he was not, of course, the chessmeister that his passport had alleged; likely he had been an intelligence agent all his career, trained and experienced in situations exactly like this. Which would justify his outrage at being sent a cub like her to bring him safely out, where his status should have promised him someone equally adept.

"I expect they got ahead of us," she said, trying to recapture something, a hint of momentum, a suggestion of still being in charge. "It's a fair guess, that we would head for the railway station; perhaps they had watchers here all along, in case they lost us on the way. I'm not sure why they're suddenly trying to kill us, but –"

"We must go back," he said. "Go back and try again, a different way. Call for help, call Colpert, have him come and take us out."

They could do that, she supposed, if she could get them away somehow from here. Hole up in a hotel somewhere – not the Blue Dolphin! – and telephone her supervisor. Betray herself, betray him too, admit she's in a hole and ask for someone better. Ask for the best. The Russian might be right: it might be the only move left to her now. He might even be right that she was never competent for this mission, only over-confident.

On the other hand...

"No," she said fixedly. More than determined, absolute. "We've come this far; we'll go the rest of the way." *I got you into this, I'll get you out.* She, Rowany Angelica Marten de Vere, scion of a noble house (albeit one overly supplied with siblings of the male gender) and product of the finest education on three planets. Two out of the three. She would try, at least. Give it her best shot. If this failed – well, then she could think again. Creep away if necessary, tail between her legs, not her father's daughter after all. Just a girl, as her brothers had always so delighted in explaining.

Meanwhile...

She licked dry chapped lips with a dry tongue that didn't seem to help at all, propped herself on her elbows, thrust fingers into the corners of her mouth and whistled, sharp and shrill. Two notes, no more. She'd learned this from Tommie, who had picked it up never-ask-where. It was the alley children's most basic, most urgent signal, *can you help?*

A chorus of answering whistles came it seemed from all over: from behind them, from ahead of them, from the roofs overhead. She hadn't thought, but of course railway marshalling yards would be infested, especially where they lay congruent with docks.

"What is that?" her companion growled, ever discontent.

"Wait. Watch."

In honesty, she had no idea what would follow. What could children do, against guns? And what could she do, except lie here and wonder?

Lying here was becoming exceedingly cold. Or perhaps that was fear, making her shudder against the frozen ground?

No, she decided. It was definitely the cold. And there was no comfort to be had from the Russian. Had she thought him sullen or out of temper before? Perhaps that was only the way his face fell, and no signifier of his inner mood. Now he seemed not frightened so much as entirely furious. He crawled over the ice until they were lying head to head and said it all again, that they must go back, that they must retreat and contact her superiors and have a new plan, a better plan, *a better agent* quite clearly implied.

She didn't think it was herself that he was angry at, though there seemed no sense in that: whose fault was this, if not her own? Still, she was trying to muster arguments she didn't have against a retreat that ought to be inevitable. She lifted her head – just to seem more certain, or more emphatic, something

– and had no idea what she was going to say and then blessedly didn't need to say anything, because she was forestalled by someone's screaming.

It was swift and shrill and very male, and followed by a tumble of curse-words – not all of which she understood – in English and Russian both.

"We have help in high places," she said when she could breathe again, when she was sure mistress of her voice, not about to betray herself.

"Again, please?"

They probably shouldn't move for another minute or two. She settled herself a little more comfortably and said, "There's not a child living wild in this city who doesn't have a catapult in their back pocket. This time of year, they don't even need to carry ammunition. A chunk of ice is perfect, and ice is everywhere. They like to shoot down from rooftops, for the shelter of the parapets and the quick getaway and maybe a little help from gravity, I don't know. Like peasants defending a castle wall, shoot and duck, peek out and shoot again."

"Even against gunfire?" He sounded exasperated, more than disbelieving.

"I don't suppose they've run up against a gun before, not one used in anger – but I don't suppose they'd think twice. I don't believe they did think twice. On their own territory, in defence of a friend, two friends? Shoot and duck, and see what happens next."

What happened next was another rifle shot, that she heard clearly this time because she was listening for it while she was talking, dreading it, expecting it. Now here it was, and it seized her heart in cold hard fingers as she waited for a cry, a dying fall, the thud of a starveling body come to ground. The absolute inevitability of guilt, self-blame, nightmares.

All she heard, though, was whistles and war-whoops from her feral battalion, followed by a patter like hail, which must have been a whole volley of ice-pellets flung down in derision. Now it was the men below who were yelping, crying out, cursing. Trying no doubt to find shelter from that stinging onslaught. Trying and failing, by the certain sound of it.

"Just a warning shot. Only goes to show."

"To show what?"

"That they have no idea what they're dealing with. Welcome to Mars, gentlemen. We don't frighten easily." She was proud of her troops, even as she worried for them, even as she prayed. "All that noise is safe to bring someone, though. Railway police, I know they have a station here. They'll think they're only coming out to run off some hoodlums, but…"

But if they found themselves faced with armed men, and were carrying nothing sterner than a truncheon, there might yet be blood shed tonight; and hers would still be the responsibility, even if she felt it less acutely. Children must inevitably lie more heavily on the conscience than officers in uniform, who ought to know what they were at. Except that these officers would have no idea; and if there was whistle-code for kids, can you warn off the bobbies? She didn't know. Besides, hers was the responsibility; she ought to take it. She ought to get between the police and the gunmen – only she couldn't think of a way to do it without inviting more bullets and making everything worse, because she and her charge were the targets here, after all.

Still, she couldn't just take advantage of the confusion to sneak him out of range and into safety, not with lives at risk. She needed… something, something else, something more, and didn't know what it was.

Yes, she did.

The simple *au secours* was not the only whistle-call she'd learned from Tommie. Here was another. Two short bursts, one long: it spoke intimately to one half of the street, but boys would understand it too.

If they were trained – and what boys were not soon trained by the girls obliged to live with them? – they would come running, because the call meant *help, assault, beware!* It meant *a man, men, pursuit!* Put simply, it meant *damsel in distress!* Put more coarsely, it meant *rape!* And it was sure, was guaranteed to bring any girl in hearing – street urchin or shop girl, mannequin or kennel-maid or cook, anyone who knew the call – and boys too, a great mob of boys, all territorial issues or disputes let lie for the duration while they swarmed to the rescue of one of their own.

Rowany wasn't honestly in fear of that kind of assault. Privately she thought that there was precious little left in her that was any kind of damsel; and if she met with anything distressing she'd been trained to respond without mercy, without ruth. Still; with shots actually fired, whether or not she'd been the target, she felt entitled to raise the hue and cry. With a bullet passing so very, very close to her head. She'd be as damsel as the situation needed, as distressed as they come. Perhaps she was only offering more hostages to fortune, bringing more children hurtling across clan lines into an ugly danger that was none of their concern, they who lived such ugly lives already. She was gambling on the ferocity of street children in general and girls in particular, where instincts of survival are moulded into instincts of attack. Gambling their lives against that ferocity. The female of this known species, *yes, Mr Kipling*, more deadly by a distance. They had to be. By the time the railway police could get here, responding late and slow as Authority always does, she hoped – and hoped that she had reason to hope – that they would find nothing *to* find, bar a couple of foreigners with dubious papers dragging each other away at the best limp they could achieve.

Her own foreigner – well, she could vouch for his papers, at least, she'd rarely seen better. Vouch for his, while flourishing her own. Those should serve to gag an inquisitive railway officer, and his superiors too. Stamped with the imprimatur of the Service, and this particular department of the Service, her papers would win her access and a hearing anywhere on Mars – well, human Mars, anywhere on Charter lands – and be almost as good on Earth, wherever the British writ yet ran.

Not that she deserved any such golden ticket, as she cowered here on the ice and summoned kids to fight for her. If her supervisor saw her – if Colpert saw her now...!

Actually, she thought her supervisor would nod

approvingly. She was doing exactly the right thing, by the book, expending casual assets to secure her mission and her prize. Colpert, she thought, would feel differently, whatever the book might say. Not that he'd speak to her about it – she was far too lowly, and not in his chain of command except morally, spiritually, absolutely – but he'd know. He'd read the reports, he'd hear accounts. Perhaps for the first time he would know her name, and with it her disgrace. He was the arbiter, the agent's agent, the perfect exemplar of the breed, and she was letting him down.

Before she knew it, she was standing up. It was ridiculous, with a rifleman out there. At least one, and who knew how many others, who might also be rallying to the sound of shots? It wasn't she who should feel flattered by such attentions, such expenditure of resources, but she did wonder just how important a defector her Uncle Vasiliy might turn out to be, if the Tsar was putting so much into his recapture.

Stupid, then, to risk him; stupid to take any chances at all with his skin or her own; nevertheless, here she was. Standing forth and holding out a hand to him, to help him up in his turn. Unarmed and ignorant, exposed, and none the less.

"What are you thinking?" he growled, prepared now to turn his unexpected anger onto her.

I'm thinking we shouldn't lurk in shelter while children, strangers, fight on our behalf. I'm thinking we should lend a hand. Nice Martian girls didn't box or wrestle or throw stones, but she wasn't that nice and her brothers were just downright nasty. She'd learned a lot even before she went to school, more before Oxford. The hockey pitch was no place for nice girls. And since then she'd had training, so much training, so many physical arts and sciences. None of them had taught her how to face an armed man bare-handed at a rifle's distance, but even so. Nice girls didn't hide from their responsibilities, or draw others into a danger they weren't willing to face themselves.

The air was shrill with whistles as she marched the Russian determinedly down a path between two warehouses, the way the bullet had come in search of her. Whistles and shouts, overhead and all around, echoing bewilderingly off high blank walls. Then another gunshot, and a high wavering cry, and she thought she was too late; then there was a figure in front of her, oozing through a gap in the masonry surely too narrow for a human body to fit, and in one hand it held a rifle.

Absolutely, then, she was too late. Heroism is

ridiculous when it comes behind the need, when the deed has been done by other hands. This stick-figure creature, too thin and stretched even for Mars, flourished the weapon in triumph. "Dropped it and ran," they offered in economical report. "Well, dropped it and hobbled," with an unexpected giggle. "Didn't want to explain this to the rozzers. Trouble enough explaining anyway, so much blood and bruises. What'ya whistle for?"

"For you, for this," she said. Apparently brevity was catching. "Rescue from that," with a nod at the rifle. "Those men meant to kill us."

"Yeah." The little face twisted in thought, the narrow shoulders shrugged at last: not mine to judge, whether or not Rowany had misused the system. "You gonna pay? Toll's due."

"We paid before. Skates, at the stairway."

"Those got you in, and welcome so. This? This is extra."

"Rifle covers that." She was almost – almost – sure that her interlocutor was a girl. At this point, it frankly made no difference to either of them.

"This? This is for you," and she – yes, call her she – held it out with a kind of urgent contempt. "We keep it, some fool's gonna use it."

"You could sell it."

72

"And then everyone knows we're trading guns, and then we have a heap of trouble all around. No thanks. You take it, pay us for the rescue, not the gun, and get you gone."

Definitely a girl, then. A boy would have known all those arguments and kept it anyway. What was she, fourteen perhaps? And so wise already, to see the lengths and shadows of the future? When found, make a note of. The first interest of the hidden world is recruitment: that had been stressed, again and again down the years. Likely prospects were to be passed up the line; instructions were to be waited for, but friendship could be cultivated without licence and without commitment. It might come to nothing; there might be many reasons to leave this girl where she was, uncontacted and feral; but it was always worth asking, and always worth the effort.

"What's your name?" she asked accordingly, casually, as she took the rifle. Both hands were briefly busy, removing the magazine and opening the bolt to be sure the rifle was unloaded; all her attention was clearly focused on her work, which left the girl free to think it over.

At length, "Bee," she muttered.

"Hullo, Bee. I'm Rowany, but you can call me Ro. Are you the queenpin around here?"

"Well, yeah. I suppose."

Rowany supposed so too. Clearly it was Bee who made decisions for her clan. A couple of boys had emerged warily behind her, but they were holding back: lieutenants, aides-de-camp, nothing more.

"Good. I don't have much money on me just now" – a lie, but one told in everyone's best interest, maybe – "so I'll have to give you something on deposit, and come back later to settle up."

Bee scowled, and indicated the silent Russian with a jerk of her head. "What about him?"

"He's got nothing except a long history, an interesting future and a target on his back in the meantime. I'll tell you all about it when I come. Look, here's my purse, with all the coins I have on me," and that at least was true. Everything else she had was paper. And coins would be easier to divide among Bee's followers, and easier for any of them to spend. A street kid with a banknote was an open invitation to all kinds of trouble. "Take this and scram, before the police arrive."

As it happened, her coin purse also held her newly-minted calling cards. Handing it over wholesale was a spontaneous back-up plan she was secretly rather pleased with. If she didn't make it back here in reasonably short order – or if she couldn't find this particular gang when she came, which was always possible; clans warred one with another, territories shifted, allegiances could be broken as swiftly as they were made – then she was tolerably certain that Bee would come in search of her. She'd baited two hooks – money, and a story – and left two possible ways to bite. That was enough for now.

The Russian's scowl was momentous, as she tramped him across the marshalling yards. Halfway over – keeping virtuously within the white lines, where wooden boards made a pathway over and between the tracks, so they were really hardly trespassing at all – a sudden hail seemingly from nowhere brought them to a swift and obedient halt.

Two men stepped out from the shadow of a wagon heaped high with redcoal. Uniforms and helmets, clearly police; she held the rifle out one-handed, high and wide.

"Just lay the gun down, sir, if you would. And keep your hands where I can see them."

Not that the two men could do anything much

between them, if she ignored that and drew a pistol and shot them both as they approached. Instead of that, she set the rifle at her feet and started talking, slowly and clearly, even before they reached her.

"My name is Rowany de Vere, and I'm with the Colonial Service. I can give you my supervisor's telephone number to confirm that. Or, wait, my office number's on my card…"

…and she'd just given all her cards away, in one reckless gesture. Storing up treasure in heaven, perhaps; leaving herself exposed here on Mars. Not that there was anything in any way official about the cards, but they looked convincing, and a call to the office would yield up any amount of confirmation.

"Is that right, miss? Sorry for calling you 'sir' before, but it's hard to tell in leathers, from a distance. And who's your gentleman friend?"

The question didn't seem to carry any connotations, despite its wording. She thought she liked this policeman. He was properly cautious, properly courageous, not impertinent and not leaping to awkward conclusions. She hoped. Certainly not stooping to innuendo.

"He's under my protection," she said, just to show that she could play word-games too, and to see if the officer smiled. If he could smile. He did, briefly; well, all right, then. Oh, and she'd given Uncle Vasiliy her card, hadn't she? He ought to have it yet.

"Your armed protection, miss?"

"Oh – no, the rifle's not ours. Not mine. Someone was taking pot-shots at us; I expect that's what you heard. Lord only knows why they'd do that, but we yelled a lot, and I suppose we scared them off. They left this behind as a trophy. I've unloaded it for you."

"For us, miss?"

"Well, yes. I'm afraid you'll have to take charge of it. Not much point writing anything up, to be honest, because that's all we can tell you; we didn't see who it was at all, and they'd scarpered before help had a chance of coming. But we can't take a rifle with us on the train, it'll only attract notice that I'd rather avoid, thanks. If it worries you, turn it in to my office; they'll take care of the thing. Uncle Silly, could you give the officer my card? The one I gave you, before?"

She meant to add a warning – move slowly, keep your hands in sight – but no need. He extracted the card from an inner pocket with two careful fingers, the consummate professional. Where had he learned that – a Russian equivalent of her own training, in some dacha outside St Petersburg? Or more directly, the way Bee might have learned it, the natural caution of the street coming face to face with Authority?

There wouldn't be any point in asking. All this time, he'd been the very opposite of forthcoming. Since he first saw her, really; since he realised that he'd been sent a girl. She was both young and female, two gross faults that he seemed unable to get past. Essentially, she was Not Colpert, and hence not the saviour he was looking for. Ah, well.

Still talking to the officers, she said, "Actually, there's something else you could help me with, if you would. Those men may not be the only people watching for us, and I'd like to get away unseen. We have a compartment reserved on the sleeper to NV; is there any way to smuggle us aboard covertly?"

"We might be able to manage that, miss. And we could keep an eye out for these watchers of yours, too."

"Don't do anything to attract their attention," she said, meaning *please don't, they're exactly what I'm trying to save you from.* "They're armed, remember. And willing to shoot at the first provocation," which had been apparently the first sight of her Russian, unless it was herself. "Besides, if they see you acting protectively, they'll know instantly whom you're protecting, and you might as well hang a flag from the train saying 'They're on this one'."

That won her another pinched smile, and, "I do see what you mean, miss. All right, we'll be careful. Though we do patrol the platforms at busy times, and this is busy now. The NV sleeper, you say? Well, then. That's Platform Eight, and it'll be switching track to run along beside the milk train at Fifteen. I'll have a word with the signalmen, have them hold it there for a couple of minutes. That won't upset anybody's timetable. Meanwhile we'll put you on the milk train – that's not boarding for hours yet, so no one's going to be watching there – and when the time comes, when the sleeper pulls up alongside, you can step straight across from the one to the other, and no one any the wiser. If you think you can manage, miss? It'll be a stretch, but I'll tell the conductor to have an eye out for you…"

"No. Don't tell anyone, please. I'm sure we can manage. It always seems frighteningly close, when one train passes another. And the sleeper has those handy whatchacall'ems, the open areas at the end of every carriage, where the gentlemen" – and not a few ladies of her acquaintance, because no right-thinking Martian woman was going to allow mere men to claim that kind of privilege – "step out to smoke their cigars after dinner, though I'm sure they're not supposed to. We can hop aboard there, and look as if we were just passing along from the next carriage. That's splendid. Thank you so much."

He eyed her a little dubiously, but her brilliant smile and the authority of her calling card between them muted him. He collected his silent mate with a jerk of his helmeted head, and they led a weaving way between tracks and wagons empty and full, carriages seemingly abandoned in mid-yard, locomotives long gone cold. Occasionally they paused to let a shunter or a full freight train go by; the policemen both had a way of standing that signalled their awareness of the oncoming engine, their certainty that they were safe and clear, even the care they were taking to keep these ignorant civilians out of danger. The engine drivers must have been long familiar with these men and their signals; they worked their steam-whistles once as a matter of form, came on at a cautious pace – because civilians can never be trusted, after all, where a man's profession is at stake – and waved cheerily as they passed by.

Looking back, Rowany found herself quite bewildered as to where they were in the vast yards, or in relation to any parts she knew of old. That was balm to her soul. This meandering route with its shifting lines of sight must make it all but impossible to track them even from a height, never mind on the ground.

The policemen knew where they were going. Of course they did. That was axiomatic: *if you want to know the way, ask a policeman*. They weren't necessarily much use for anything else – her new Service was deeply contemptuous of the bobbies and all their works, and she was ever ready to absorb the ethos and attitudes of a fresh cohort, first at school and then at Oxford and now here: perhaps that was a fault, loyalty taken too far, sign of a frivolous and superficial character? – but for guidance through unknown territory, there really was no one better than a local bobby.

Platform Fifteen: Rowany knew it well, though not of course from this angle, approaching across the tracks. It served a branch line, and therefore stood apart from the main concourse under its monumental arch of roof. At the far end of that branch line was the town of Terminus, and on the lake above the town stood the Crater School, where Rowany had spent seven delightful, delighted years. She couldn't count how many times she'd changed trains here. Once or twice, let it be admitted, she and her friends had been having so much fun passing time here in Marsport between one train and the next they had allowed a little too much time to pass, and missed their intended connection, and so had to catch this very milk train instead, and wash up on the bleak unwelcoming school steps at a shockingly early hour of the morning, and have to face a bleak unwelcoming interview with the headmistress before they could even fortify themselves with breakfast.

Even at their most wicked, though, they had never dodged across the tracks to get here, with actual trains steaming back and forth around them. So they'd never had to climb into a compartment from the trackside ballast, three feet lower than the platform. It was a stretch even for young Martian legs, never mind a squat and heavy Russian encumbered with all the wear of winter.

Still, he hauled himself up and in, once she'd opened the compartment door. Martian gravity might have helped, though he was presumably used to Venusian by now, which was not so different. Scientists were still arguing about that, the last she heard, why the gravity on Mars was not as light as theory and size suggested. No matter. Here they were, on an empty train – it would fill up in an hour or so, country families heading home after an exciting day in town, shopping and seeing Father Christmas in a department store and all the lights everywhere and the animated window displays and the pantomime – waiting to make a daring switch onto another, while enemies no doubt patrolled the platforms in hunt of them. Enemies with guns, willing to shoot without warning. Willing to kill. It was a hard thought to hold on to, that a marginally better aim would have left her dead back there. She had done her own training with rifle and handgun, of course, and she liked to believe she would use them as scrupulously in action as she did in the firing-range, but none of her instructors had given any time to the other end of the exchange. Perhaps they should; perhaps that was something else to mention to Mr Colpert when the chance arose, that every agent-in-training should come under fire at some point, just to find out how they fared.

Privately, she felt that she had fared tolerably well, then and since. It was hard to keep in her head, perhaps, but that was just as well in the circumstances. Let it go for now, worry about it later if she needed to. In the meantime, she and her charge were still alive, still free, and at least one pair of assailants was disarmed and out of the game, at least for now. The others – assuming that there were others, which she had to do but was confident of in any case – might even have lost their trail entirely. At least she felt entitled to hope so, though she would absolutely assume the opposite, all the way to New Victoria.

Thinking about New Victoria, the journey, the welcome she'd receive on arrival – *on delivery*, she thought, a little rudely – she could almost manage not to think about what was left to do beforehand, the secret switch of trains. Almost. It was there in her head, though, like the fragment of a tune she couldn't stop whistling, running over and over again: just how they'd accomplish it, and how well it would work, how they'd be completely invisible from any of the platforms no matter how many watchers there were out there – and there really did seem to be a lot, even an unwarranted amount to pursue one turncoat. They were risking so much, throwing so many agents into the chase, he must have some deadly level of secrets to sell if they valued him this highly.

Oh.

If the Russians valued him this highly, and couldn't spot him, couldn't spot them, rather – him and her together – on any of the platforms, it would be an easy guess to look for the train to New Victoria. Where else would a hunted fugitive go, than to the provincial capital where all manner of institutions stood by to defend and succour him?

What chance that they wouldn't have an agent, perhaps many of these agents they seemed so willing to spend, already booked on the sleeper to NV? They wouldn't have made a move against their target on the platform anyway, with so many people around to see. No, the train itself would be their target. And likely they'd have bought a passenger manifest from some willing bribable clerk, and taken note of the young woman travelling with her putative uncle, and matched that against what they already knew...

She needed to stop thinking that way, before he read too much of what was in her mind. Agents needed lessons in poker-face, she decided, as much as they did in psychology.

"Do you play Vint?" she asked abruptly.

"Vint? Of course I play Vint, I am Russian. How can you know about Vint?"

"Three brothers," she said briefly, "and a boarding-school education."

She took a pack of cards out of her pocket, and began to shuffle.

"Vint needs four," he objected derisively. "It cannot be played with two!"

"Yes, it can. We'll play two dummies, half-open. It's a method we worked out for ourselves, my best friend and I, for when all the boys were busy doing boy-things or we found ourselves with an unexpected free period. Arranging foursomes can be tricky, either in families or at school, but twos are always easy. And it works for three as well, if you just play one dummy. Look, I'll show you. We'll play out one contract with everything face-up, so you can see how it works…"

He still wanted to insist that two English schoolgirls could not possibly have transformed a Russian tradition into anything worth the having. But they had time to kill, and talking about anything that mattered would become impossible as soon as anyone joined them in their compartment; and as soon as she set the cards down on the half-table beneath the window and began to demonstrate the layout, he was suddenly engaged. She'd been counting on that. He must surely be a games player, after all, if he could even try to pass as one of a chess entourage; and she knew games players of old.

"...So you are making a contract with yourself?"

"I suppose you are, yes. I know it sounds a bit silly – but you're competing with me, and you can only see half your dummy's hand, and so can I, so..."

And so they played one open hand through, debating rules and possibilities, good plays and poor; and then they played for true. And at length a train pulled up on the track beside, and stood there awhile, hissing and wheezing, and he didn't lift his head from his cards except to eye her as he bid a contract; and it was already whistling and pulling away when he jerked up and said, "Was not that –?"

"Yes," she said placidly.

"But we should –" Even now, apparently he wanted to jump out and run after it.

"No," she said, laughing as she seized his sleeve to be sure of him. "We really shouldn't."

He sat down, glowering, suspicious as ever. "I do not understand."

"No, because I didn't explain. I was slow to see the difficulty myself," *and then I just chose not to have the inevitable argument. Better to ask forgiveness than permission, and God bless the Crater School for teaching me that, though of course they never intended to. Lessons for Naughty Middles, a Primer: handed down from previous generations, and I swallowed it whole...* "Even if those railway policemen weren't found and bribed," she went on, explaining rather than asking for anything, "which I'm afraid is all too likely, for they're notoriously ill-paid and notoriously corrupt in consequence – but even if they were honest examples of the breed, it seemed all too likely that those chasing you would put men on the sleeper, and then go from berth to berth until they found us. On a moving train, there's nowhere to hide and nowhere to run."

"So instead we are on a static train?" he said poisonously.

"On a train where they will never think to look for us," she said. Still keeping that magisterial Head Girl calm. "Either they were told we'd be on the sleeper, or else they will have divined it, because of course we'd want to go to New Victoria. Either way, they can search that train from end to end and find neither of us, and will have no way to communicate that until it arrives at NV, for it doesn't stop at all along the way." Unlike this one, which would stop everywhere. She was perhaps not quite as sanguine as she seemed, as she went on, "So we'll do what no one expects, and ride the milk train out to Terminus, and once we're there – well. Once we're there, I'll introduce you to a side of the Red Raj that you never thought you'd see."

"The terminus? Where is the terminus for this train?"

"Oh, I'm sorry. The town's called Terminus, because it's so far out in the wilds. Two canals end there, and so does this railway line. It's right on the edge of Charter territory; there's nowhere farther to go."

"And yet you take me there, where we have no option except to come back?"

"Oh, yes. Yes, very definitely I take you there. We'll be safe there, I promise. You'll see."

And then, deliberately infuriating, she would say nothing more; and he must be content to fume silently as two voluble farmers' wives and their equally silent dairymaids came in from a day's marketing, begging the gentleman's pardon but all the compartments were filling up now as they always did, and they would only be going as far as Whittlebury Halt, not halfway up the valley...

The gentleman all too clearly did mind, but there was little he could do; and Rowany was not in the least inclined to help him. He refused to play another hand of cards: very well. She dealt out patience for herself, and played that through with as much inscrutability as she could manage, while he sat and stewed in impotence, and she wondered once again why his former masters would be so keen to spend so many men – and perhaps women too – to track him down. What did he know, what *could* he know? The names of every Russian agent in Marsport, heavens, every Russian agent on Mars would hardly be worth saving, if most of them were exposed anyway in the hunt for the man who could reveal them.

Time passed, and distance with it. Slow time, slow distance. The women left at last, but neither Rowany nor her charge were in any mood to speak now. They were both drowsy, and both kept from sleeping by the constant sounds and motion as the train hissed to a halt, doors slammed, whistles blew, movement began again in a series of jerks and groans. No one more joined them in their compartment – this outward run was all about dropping people off, as near to their homes as a train could manage – but there were no more cards now, and no more conversation.

Only the lights of the little stations interrupted the long dark, bar the occasional lantern on a wagon wending home or a gleam from the window of a distant farmstead. Rowany watched them pass, wondering vaguely about the lives they bespoke: did that light mean anxious parents up with a sickly child, or was it a silent guide for an errant lover, or a sleepless parson bending over his books, anxious about Sunday when he must preach before the bishop...?

Mostly, though, she barely thought at all. She only watched the darkness slide away, trying to seem unperturbed, finding it hard even to remember *confident and competent* under the constant critical glare of her companion. He had no leeway in him, seemingly; anything he had not approved must be rejected, and he most emphatically had not approved her and apparently never would.

The Tsar's court at St Petersburg and Russia generally were old news, more or less, but she knew little enough – heavens, the Department entire knew embarrassingly little – about current conditions on Venus. A convict colony, the new Siberia: it was hard for agents to penetrate, harder to escape. Few women were sent there, she did know that; but even so, to the fiercely independent mind of a young Martian woman, his attitude seemed so out of time, it was almost a parody of itself. Even on Venus there must be women who worked, women who took risks, women who took charge. Surely, there must?

Another man she might ask, but not this one. Not in the face of his absolute contempt. If things had gone otherwise, if her first declared plan had worked better, he might have mellowed; he might even have been willing to talk. But he knew that she was scrambling now, improvising hastily to cover for both misfortunes and mistakes. Improvising poorly, she worried: every move she took, she seemed to have been second-guessed already. No one could fairly expect her to have anticipated such a wholesale mobilisation of forces, but he had no interest in being fair;. She knew that every twist and turn she made counted against her in his mind, even if it bought them time, even if it promised freedom.

She might have been over-hasty in that promise. That was another worry. She'd shown no signs yet of out-thinking the opposition. Maybe his contempt was entirely justified; maybe she would lose this roll as she had the last and the one before that. Maybe she was leading him into one more trap, without any of the escape options she'd found in the city. She'd been lucky thus far – that bullet, so close, she could still feel the wind of it like a line drawn along her cheek – but luck was ever fickle.

Still. Even more than Marsport, this was her own home territory they were heading into; and her best advantage held true yet, that she was native-born and they were not. If she couldn't outwit strangers who knew nothing of her people nor her land, she didn't deserve the title on her calling card nor the ever-present whisper of it in her head that thrilled her so, all the more for what it did not say: Rowany de Vere. Of the Colonial Office. It might mean nothing at all – a clerical job, a typewriter and a shorthand pad – but in fact it meant so much, and it was so much to live up to. She'd hoped to make a better fist of things, her first time out.

Still. Here they were, and there was the first hint of coming day, the sky turning slowly caramel beyond the mountains, a promise of the bright beloved tawny with its fierce speck of sun. That was one promise that Mars would keep, with or without her.

She shivered under a sudden sense of foreboding, and tried to shrug it off; tried to listen through all the noises of the train to the silence of the sun's rising, the first stirrings of birdsong, the –

– the sound of an airship engine overhead.

Just for a minute, she persuaded herself that she was being alarmist. But once her mind had identified the sound it was unmistakable, inescapable – and it wasn't passing by, it wasn't pulling away. That Zeppelin was hanging directly above the train, tracking it, keeping it company. Not troubling to hide its purpose.

She might be a trained agent, confident and competent – but she was still human underneath all that. Still Martian, composed half of curiosity and half of derring-do. Of course she slid the window down, of course she leaned out and peered upward. She might have been vaguely hopeful that perhaps they couldn't see her down here in the valley shadow, where no light had reached – but she didn't think to turn off the compartment lamp before she looked out, so no doubt she had just absolutely advertised her presence here. Still, it was fairly clear that had been divined already. There it was, hanging directly over the train at no great height, the sleek black cigar silhouetted against the lightening sky, its motor putt-puttering with an occasional flare of burning dust to speak of how old the engine was, because modern airships all burned redcoal oil rather than the rock itself.

There could be no reason for an airship so assiduously to follow a train, unless those aboard were interested in passengers or cargo in those particular carriages. And this wasn't even the milk train yet, though everyone called it that; there was no real cargo, only housewives' gathered packages and depleted purses. It beggared belief that there might be another party in pursuit of someone else aboard, a party with the resources to recruit an airship pilot and his machine. She made no attempt to deceive herself: this was yet one more unfathomable response from the Russians in chase of her and her charge, one more overreaction. One more failure on her part, no doubt, not to have anticipated this. If there had been agents on the sleeper, perhaps they'd pulled the communication cord and jumped out, once they were sure that their targets were not aboard that train. Perhaps they'd run to the nearest public telephone and called their controller, who had promptly sent more men after the only other train to have left Marsport this late, in the only conveyance capable of catching it...

That must have been it. Even her febrile imagination couldn't conceive of multiple airships chasing multiple trains, watching at every station for signs of those they hunted. No, one way or another the chase had narrowed down to this train; perhaps now it had narrowed down to this carriage, perhaps they knew at last that they were right.

Very well, then. Assume that she and her companion had been discovered once again, and carry on. At least she knew exactly where she was going. They could hover and watch at every station between here and Terminus, they'd see nothing to interest them. Unless she tried a feint, two well-wrapped figures scuttling through the lamplight, then sneaking back to board the train again in shadow...?

No. She'd been out-thought all down the line, and outplayed too: very well. It was time to play to her strengths, in a landscape she knew intimately, in a world entirely her own. They would ride this train to the end of the line, and then go on from there.

FOUR

The sun had still not risen over the mountains by the time they reached Terminus, betraying its imminence via no more than a few butterscotch streaks. The train pulled into the station, wheezing and blowing; Rowany gathered her companion and all his traps with a stern eye, opened the compartment door and stepped out boldly onto the platform.

There was an awning here overhead, but she had no doubt that the airship was still up there. By now, she had decided simply to assume they knew who she was, and where therefore she was going. Whether or not they could see her would make no difference now.

Accordingly, she led her charge through the station to another platform, where another train awaited: this one small, unusual in design, already steam-up.

If she huffed with relief to find it still running in this depth of winter, this depth of holiday, she was careful not to let on. Instead she greeted the platform guard blithely, insouciantly, as an old friend: "Joe! Lovely to see you again. Nice to see things haven't totally fallen apart in my absence. Funicular ready to go, is she?"

"Miss Rowany! Well, you're a sight for sore eyes, I must say! Back to visit your old haunts, are you? She'll be away in ten minutes, miss, yes. Milk and mail, as ever: the school and the San never really close, do they? Besides, it's Christmas. There's any number of packages aboard, for those poor souls who can't leave the rim."

He meant the patients, she knew, at the famous Sanatorium that fought constantly with all the diseases peculiar to Mars. Sometimes, she knew all too well, it was equally true of the schoolgirls whose parents were gone to Earth or sick at home or visiting elsewhere, so that their daughters were obliged to spend the holidays at school. Rowany herself had done it, often and often. The staff went out of their way to make sure the girls enjoyed themselves thoroughly – rather to the detriment, newly-adult Rowany realised, of the staff's own holidays – but still, it was always hard to miss out on time at home. Especially at Christmas.

She tipped Joe handsomely, as ever; it never hurt to lubricate a friendship. Not till they were comfortably settled in a long-familiar compartment aboard the funicular did the Russian ask, "And where are you taking me now?"

"Up to the rim, Uncle Vasiliy. The sun should just be coming over the crater wall when we get there, it's that late at this time of year; the near side will still be in shadow, but you'll see the light come rushing over the water towards us, it's a beautiful sight…"

No one, so far as she knew, was listening, but even so: *never break your cover story. Make it real, for as long as it needs to last.* She didn't think that even he was listening to her answer. Certainly she was not really listening to herself, nor to him, nor anything except the buzzing airship overhead.

Was it alert to some signal from the ground, to confirm that she and her companion had taken this train onwards? Perhaps; it might have landed a man ahead of the milk train's coming. Or the driving force in that gondola above was merely certain of his quarry's next move: predictable, perhaps inevitable, this run to known ground.

Nevertheless. She was still not going to rethink, try to double back, seek help from the stationmaster at the other end of the line. This was her task, and she was well fitted for it, and she would win through with her charge and her mission intact. She was quite determined on that. *Rowany can do anything if she puts her mind to it.* That was a chance remark she'd overheard unintentionally, back when all – well, almost all – of her eavesdropping was unintentional, when she was an honourable schoolgirl. Given that its source had been her old headmistress, who was then and was still somewhat of a goddess to her, and that she had been a ridiculously impressionable adolescent at the time, she had adopted it forthwith as her eternal motto.

Very well, then. Her mind was entirely set on this, and she would see it through.

The train – they had always called it a funicular, in defiance of the staff's constant insistence that it was not – reached the lower slopes of the crater wall, and she felt the familiar jerk as the rack-and-pinion mechanism engaged. When she was a Junior, a science lesson about the system had been followed by a field trip to see it in action, a whole classful of little girls squatting by the trackside gaping at the great cogwheel beneath the strangely tilted locomotive, gasping as it steamed slowly past with the teeth locking securely one by one into the rack between the rails, shrieking as smuts from the chimney descended onto their faces and uniforms and none the less clamouring to ride up in the cab with the driver. They'd all of them ridden on the train itself by then, coming and going between school and town, but this was different.

Now it was different again, and the train had never seemed so slow, nor the sun so swift to rise. It would be properly up, and all her hopes confounded, if the driver didn't get a move on. But of course he knew of no reason to hurry; this was a milk and mail run, no more. There were no other passengers. He might not even know they were aboard at all, she and the Russian. Besides, she was only imagining the dawdle. The locomotive had always been one-paced, just as the sun was; if it went no faster than its age-old crawl, neither did it go any slower.

Up the crater wall, up and up. There was a pinion wheel beneath each car and carriage too, she knew, so that if the coupling to the locomotive broke, the train still couldn't go careering backwards down the steep slope to an inevitable doom below – but even the steady tick-tick-tick of those teeth connecting with the rack below couldn't calm her jitters now. Apparently that rifle bullet had upset something in her that she had thought long settled, a tendency to imagine grim and grisly ends to all her adventures.

Still. No need to let that show. *Competence and confidence*, yes. She would project calmness, a clear certainty that nothing important would break, including her nerve. The thought did cross her mind that a Zeppelin must make an excellent and steady platform for firing down from – but she dismissed that briskly. One bullet didn't make a war, and all this trouble – all this expense, in both money and human resources – surely meant that they weren't in the assassination business. Not yet, at least. They wanted the Russian back alive, if they could get him.

Well, let them try. He was her Uncle Vasiliy, and she was not known for giving up her relatives. Her own fate might be incidental here, but she would make damn sure – sorry, Mum! – that it would take a major incident to get the man away from her.

Here they were, pulling into the station on the crater rim at last. In honesty, it was barely more than a platform and a set of buffers, but it did have a stationmaster, even if he did spend half his day running deliveries along the coach road to the school and the Sanatorium in his old steam-wagon. There he was now, standing with a lantern held aloft against the last of the night's darkness. Like Joe below, he was an old friend of Rowany's – *a willing slave to her wickedness*, her headmistress had been heard to say, back in the days when she was a naughty Middle – and he barely blinked to see her debouch from the milk train, years after she'd left school, with a heavy middle-aged Russian in her train.

Briefly, she was disappointed to find him so stalwart in the face of what should in all decency have been a soul-shaking surprise. But then she remembered that there was a telephone line to the stationmaster's house; of course Joe had called up to warn him. Of course the two of them would have had a nice coze together, gossiping about her as they hadn't had the chance to do in years, whatever strange whim could have drawn her back at such an unearthly hour and in such curious company.

"Mr Jenkins!" He was always 'Mr Jenkins', while Joe was always Joe. Perhaps that was the difference between platform guard and stationmaster, though honestly Mr Jenkins spent far less time than Joe anywhere near actual railway property. "How are you? And the family? Still raising those prizewinning ducks...?"

And so on, a veneer of light chatter to gloss over all the strangeness of her arriving this way in this unlikely season.

At last, when she gave him the chance, he said, "You just step into my house to get warm, Miss Rowany, you and your friend, and I'll give you a ride around to the school as soon as I've got the wagon loaded. Unless you want to go all the way to the San, and see Miss Tolchard first?"

"None of us old hands ever did learn to call her Mrs Mackenzie, did we?" she said, laughing. "But no, I thought we'd take the lakeside walk, if you could just lend me that lamp of yours. I want Uncle Vasiliy to see the dawn light come over the sky and down across the water, but this side will be in the rim's shadow all the way, so we'd best have something to see by."

"Take it and welcome, Miss Rowany. If you're sure, mind. It'll be cold by the water."

"I know it. Who better? But I've never minded that; and Uncle Vasiliy is Moscow-born. We'll be fine, Mr Arthur. If I get the chance, I'll come back to see you all later on. Your children must be quite grown now, I suppose? I hope they still remember me, we were very best friends when they were little…"

Talking, talking: and reaching for the lamp as she talked, because otherwise he would hold onto it and talk himself until her current hopes were extinguished by the coming of the sun. Or else he would offer to light them all their way to the school himself, and once the offer was made he would be obliged to insist on it, however strong her demurrals. That would be worse. Already he was peering up, puzzled, trying to identify the source of the sounds he could hear. Airships were rare hereabouts, and must surely betoken some matter of importance. But neither she nor the Russian so much as glanced upwards, so he couldn't raise the question without risk of embarrassing himself; it was a case of pride with him, that he knew everything first about the doings on Lowell Crater. She was counting on that.

At last she pried the hurricane lamp from his fingers, if not the last words from her mouth; she bade him goodbye, promised again to visit his family if she had the chance, and hustled her putative uncle along the platform and away.

She really didn't need the lamp for this. Her feet knew every inch of the gravel path they followed, down through a cleft in the rock of the rim proper, to where the crater lake lay dark and still and entirely frozen over. No snow here, and no wind: only the bitter chill lying across her shoulders like a weight, hard to breathe against.

She tucked her arm through the Russian's, just to be sure of him, and steered him to the right.

"This path goes all the way around the lake, but we don't. You see those lights up ahead? That's where we're going. Twenty minutes' brisk walk, no more."

"It looks like a castle," he said doubtfully.

"That's right. A fake castle, of course; it was built as a hotel, no more than a hundred years ago. It's been a school ever since the war. We always used to argue whether it should have been called the Castle School, rather than the Crater School. You'll see it better any minute; there's a gap in the crater wall right there, so the sun'll find it before ever it finds us here in the shelter of the wall. Look, you can see the shape of it already, more than just those lighted windows…"

"I can see the airship too," he said pointedly. "And they can see us, because you asked for that light."

"That's right," she said easily.

"Put it out!"

"No. I want them to know exactly where we are."
It was a gamble – but she knew the territory, and
whoever was commanding that Zeppelin did not. If
they were lucky, neither did the pilot. Even the Mars-
born, even the experienced airman that she had to
assume at the controls was likely to be familiar with
city and canal navigation, and likely to assume that
the same conditions obtained even out here in the
far reaches of the colony. She hoped.

She too could see the airship clearly now, a
silhouette like a cannon-shell turning slowly to aim
itself directly at them. Coming closer and closer,
lower and lower. A cannon-shell with feet jutting out
below, feet on stilts at a perky angle.

She stood stock-still, despite the cold. Held her
breath, held his arm with both of hers, held on to
hope though it squirmed like an unwilling cat and
nearly fled her.

Down and down, lower and lower – to a perfect
touchdown, neatly in the centre of the lake.

She exhaled, a sigh of sheer relief.

"We should run," he said, "why are we standing
here? We should go back, perhaps that man will
shelter us..."

"No," she said. "Wait. Watch."

Watch and listen, she should have said, perhaps.
For what? For this, first and best: a groan, a creak

that reached all across the frozen lake. And then a crack, and then a fusillade of cracking; and the airship lurched abruptly, canted to the side, was suddenly aswim in a sea of broken ice.

"Everyone knows," she said, and then corrected herself, "everyone out here knows that you never land an airship on a crater lake. It's not like the canals; the ice towards the centre is always thin, it'll always break."

"It won't matter," he said. "They are designed to land on water as well as ice. They float. They can motor to where the ice is strong."

"Yes, but wait. Watch."

Don't listen. Not now.

None the less, she did. Of course she did; she was responsible for this. They had followed where she led; they had seen her make a target of herself and her companion; they had struck. Because they knew nothing, they had struck the easy way, the obvious choice that she had led them to. Really, she hadn't allowed them a choice at all.

She was responsible.

The airship lurched again, as if the water too had given way beneath its weight. Or no, not that: it was being lurched, drawn down on one side while something – just a shadow in this difficult light, but something lobsterish – was climbing up the other.

Now more than one, now many, and assailing from every side: tearing the envelope apart, crawling all over. And now here came what she had been dreading, the screams from those men trapped inside the gondola. There was no hope for them, there was no help; but still they screamed, and still she was responsible.

She stood there in silence, in tribute, and made sure that he stood too; and heard him murmur "Tovarischchi" under his breath, and understood then that he didn't know she understood Russian. She'd been careful always to speak in English, even when there was no clear need to do so. Nothing about him had ever invited confidences, friendship, anything that might have moved her to use his own native tongue.

Perhaps it was just as well.

Too soon to feel in any way triumphant. She said, "You never, ever land on a crater lake. There's always the chance of merlins. A Martian ought to have known that, even if they didn't know for sure." She, of course, had known for sure. A naiad, with her attendant nymphs; this wasn't the first airship Rowany had seen torn apart on these waters, though at least that time her crew had got out alive. Not in midwinter, when the naiad was at her hungriest and the nymphs their most desperate. They must have eaten all the fish out of the lake long since, and couldn't go foraging ashore with that cap of ice over all. This would have been a gift from Heaven. And Rowany had known, and was responsible.

She'd never killed a man before, never mind a crew of men.

"Come," she said. "We should get out of this cold."

FIVE

Later – and it was a lot later, because in all the chaos of their arrival amid the calamity on the lake, the one sure thing was that Sister Anthony had found her and scolded her and steered her straight to bed with a cup of hot milk and no doubt some sleeping-dose hidden within, without letting her tell even the beginning of her story, even to the headmistress who did most need to know – Rowany forsook the warmth and comfort of a bed in the school sanatorium, bathed and dressed and went in search of shriving.

After one brief detour, she hunted down Miss Leven in her study and confessed all, or at least all that she could under the strictures of her oath and duty. Then, rather than asking for wise counsel, penance or absolution, as she had thought to do, she asked instead for permission to use the telephone.

Her old headmistress was far less surprised by this than Rowany herself, and left her alone in the study with the instrument. Rowany's hands were shaking a little now, but she lifted the receiver and put a call through to the Department.

Once she had given her name, there were numerous clicks and buzzes on the line, and then a laconic voice said, "Colpert."

"Oh! I – I'm sorry, sir, I think we've been misconnected. I asked to speak with Mr Witherly…"

"Not at all, Miss de Vere. Witherly's here too, a little anxious about his straying lamb, but I'm delighted to hear from you. Do say, now: where exactly are you, and what is your situation?"

She started to explain again, and he interrupted her: "Yes, yes, we know where you've been. The Frost Fair, the railway, Terminus. Our last report had you on the branch line, headed for Lowell Crater. After that we have deductions but no data. Again, please, your situation?"

"I'm at the school, sir. I think we're safe now – at least, I think I am – but…"

"Safe, hmm? That's good. What of the airship that was tracking you? I confess, we were slow to pick up on that, and thought it better not to engage in pyrotechnics in the sky. I was confident that you would find a way to evade pursuit, even from the air. On your home turf, as it were. The school is not under siege, I trust?"

"Er, no, sir. I, um, led the airship into making a mistake."

A moment's pause, and then, "A fatal one?"

"Yes, sir."

"Well. I won't congratulate you, because I know that isn't a deed you want to celebrate; and I won't ask for details, though you'll need to give them to Witherly. Nevertheless, you have done sterling service for us this last day, and it won't be forgotten. How's your travelling companion?"

"Oh – that's another thing. I'm afraid I may have lost him. At least, I went by his room just now, and he isn't there. Maybe he's just exploring the castle, but… well, I don't think so. I think he's gone. Sir, I'm not sure, and this might sound stupid, but I think perhaps he wasn't quite what he claimed to be."

"Oh, he absolutely was not what he claimed to be. Well done for spotting that. How did he give himself away?"

"There was something he said – to himself, or

rather to them, the men aboard – as we saw the airship go down; but I was wondering before that. Long before that. He did keep insisting that he wanted you to come yourself, to the point where it seemed – well, more than odd, actually. And then when they fired at us down by the station, he wasn't scared so much as furious…"

"Yes. That would be the moment when he realised that he himself was expendable, if they could only get to me. He'd been told to bring me in alive, but that message might not have percolated in time to all the men they had out looking for us. That, or the rifleman was just a giddy enthusiast who thought he had me in his sights. I'm afraid you were a decoy, Miss de Vere. We knew from the beginning that this whole palaver was a trap, intended to snare me; so we thought we'd turn it around, and take the opportunity to sweep up as many as we could manage. We've been following them as they've been following you, nabbing them as you left them in your wake. Don't worry about your absconder; he'll be interested in nothing now except his own skin, and frightened men tend to make mistakes. We'll catch up with him sooner or later; he's nowhere to go. I'm sorry we couldn't tell you about all this ahead of time, but I was assured that you'd be the right person for the job, as indeed you were. It's been a very successful operation. They'll need to rebuild their network from the ground up, and this time perhaps we can stay on top of them. By the way, when you come in to see Witherly, do drop by my office afterwards, won't you? It may be that I can put you in the way of something interesting…"

Then there was Mr Witherly to talk to, all while she was still breathless; and at last, when she was done with that call, she needed something else, something less overwhelming than Colpert's voice in her head. So she picked up the telephone again and called her own home.

Her heart lifted all by itself, when she heard the voice at the other end. "Oh, Peter! I'm so glad it's you who spoke. Is that appalling smelly little Zep of yours actually airworthy at the moment?"

He laughed. "Do you need rescuing again, sister mine?"

"Yes," she said decidedly. "Yes, I do. Can you come to the school? Can you come today?"

"Surely, if I roust the kids out to help me get her

ready."

"Oh, are the boys both home too? That's even better. You must all come. Get here in time for dinner, if you can. You and I will have to sit with Miss Leven and make polite conversation, but we'll scatter the boys among the poor girls who have to stay here for Christmas. A subaltern and an officer cadet: they shall be my Christmas present to the school. Full regimentals, mind, all three of you. Wear everything. You will descend among us like gods, and the girls will scatter rose petals before your feet. It'll be terribly bad for the boys' characters, to be treated like heroes; that can be my Christmas present to them. You can stay overnight, of course, there's masses of room and Mrs Bailey's safe to have made food enough to feed a regiment. Even a regiment of boys, even our two. Then we can all go home together in the morning, and make glad the hearts of the parents thereof. Oh, but Peter? Don't even think of landing on the lake, will you? Come down on the hockey field. I wouldn't want to lose three brothers all at once, abominable though you be…"

About the Author

Chaz Brenchley has been making a living as a writer since the age of eighteen. He is the author of thrillers, fantasies, ghost stories, science fiction and more. He has also published as Daniel Fox and Ben Macallan. 2021 saw the publication of his "Best Of" collection, *Everything in All the Wrong Order*. He is currently writing girls' boarding-school stories set on Mars, Sherlock Holmes stories ditto (what? If Mars were a province of the British Empire, Sherlock would absolutely have retired there to raise his bees – and, as it happens, an apprentice), and rather too much else. His work has won multiple awards. Born and raised in Oxford, he spent his adulthood in Newcastle on Tyne, and is now experiencing his age in Silicon Valley, California.

His website is www.chazbrenchley.co.uk, and he can be found on Facebook, Ko-fi, and Patreon.

ALSO FROM NEWCON PRESS

ANIMALS – Geoff Ryman
A powerful new novel from the multiple award-winning author of *HIM*, *Was* and *The Child Garden* The chilling tale of a family caught at the heart of a terrifying and transformative epidemic; an astonishing fusion of beautiful writing and pure horror as the world we know falls apart.

The Hamlet – Joanna Corrance
A fabulous tale that dances between horror and science fiction with an added dash of weird, *The Hamlet* is a mosaic featuring the inter-linked lives of inhabitants of a very peculiar rural community during the time when 'things got strange', and shows us the consequences of that strangeness.

The Creator – Aliya Whiteley
When Phillip receives a distraught call to say that his brother is dead, he doesn't hesitate in dashing to his sister-in-law's side. Little does he imagine the tragedy and horror that awaits ors what has really happened to the genius behind ThinkBulb, the invention that changed the world.

Birdwatching at the End of the World – GW Dexter When the world ends, the pupils of Near School for Girls are forced to fend for themselves on an isolated Scottish island with limited resources, no adults, and no prospect of rescue, as they determine to survive in this new and brutal world.